The Ultimate Weapon

The Ultimate Weapon
by John W. Campbell, Jr.

Table of Contents

Chapter I

Patrol Cruiser "IP-T 247" circling out toward Pluto on leisurely inspection tour to visit the outpost miners there, was in no hurry at all as she loafed along. Her six-man crew was taking it very easy, and easy meant two-man watches, and low speed, to watch for the instrument panel and attend ship into the bargain.

She was about thirty million miles off Pluto, just beginning to get in touch with some of the larger mining stations out there, when Buck Kendall's turn at the controls came along. Buck Kendall was one of life's little jokes. When Nature made him, she was absentminded. Buck stood six feet two in his stocking feet, with his usual slight stoop in operation. When he forgot, and stood up straight, he loomed about two inches higher. He had the body and muscles of a dock navvy, which Nature started out to make. Then she forgot and added something of the same stuff she put in Sir Francis Drake. Maybe that made Old Nature nervous, and she started adding different things. At any rate, Kendall, as finally turned out, had a brain that put him in the first rank of scientists—when he felt like it—the general constitution of an ostrich and a flair for gambling.

The present position was due to such a gamble. An IP man, a friend of his, had made the mistake of betting him a thousand dollars he wouldn't get beyond a Captain's bars in the Patrol. Kendall had liked the idea anyway, and adding a bit of a bet to it made it irresistible. So, being a very particular kind of a fool, the glorious kind which old Nature turns out now and then, he left a five million dollar estate on Long Island, Terra, that same evening, and joined up in the Patrol. The Sir Francis Drake strain had immediately come forth—and Kendall was having the time of his life. In a six-man cruiser, his real work in the Interplanetary Patrol had started. He was still in it—but it was his command now, and a blue circle on his left sleeve gave his lieutenant's rank.

Buck Kendall had immediately proceeded to enlist in his command the IP man who had made the mistaken bet, and Rad Cole was on duty with him now. Cole was the technician of the T-247. His rank as Technical Engineer was practically equivalent to Kendall's circle-rank, which made the two more comfortable together.

Cole was listening carefully to the signals coming through from Pluto. "That," he decided, "sounds like Tad Nichols' fist. You can recognize that broken-down truck-horse trot of his on the key as far away as you can hear it."

"Is that what it is?" sighed Buck. "I thought it was static mushing him at first. What's he like?"

"Like all the other damn fools who come out two billion miles to scratch rock, as if there weren't enough already on the inner planets. He's got a rich platinum property. Sells ninety percent of his output to buy his power, and the other eleven percent for his clothes and food."

"He must be an efficient miner," suggested Kendall, "to maintain 101% production like that."

"No, but his bank account is. He's figured out that's the most economic level of production. If he produces less, he won't be able to pay for his heating power, and if he produces more, his operation power will burn up his bank account too fast."

"Hmmm—sensible way to figure. A man after my own heart. How does he plan to restock his bank account?"

"By mining on Mercury. He does it regularly—sort of a commuter. Out here his power bills eat it up. On Mercury he goes in for potassium, and sells the power he collects in cooling his dome, of course. He's a good miner, and the old fool can make money down there." Like any really skilled operator, Cole had been sending Morse messages while he talked. Now he sat quiet waiting for the reply, glancing at the chronometer.

"I take it he's not after money—just after fun," suggested Buck.

"Oh, no. He's after money," replied Cole gravely. "You ask him—he's going to make his eternal fortune yet by striking a real bed of jovium, and then he'll retire."

"Oh, one of that kind."

"They all are," Cole laughed. "Eternal hope, and the rest of it." He listened a moment and went on. "But old Nichols is a first-grade engineer. He wouldn't be able to remake that bankroll every time if he wasn't. You'll see his Dome out there on Pluto—it's always the best on the planet. Tip-top shape. And he's a bit of an experimenter too. Ah—he's with us."

Nichols' ragged signals were coming through—or pounding through. They were worse than usual, and at first Kendall and Cole couldn't make them out. Then finally they got them in bursts. The man was excited, and his bad key-work made it worse. "—Randing stopped. They got him I think. He said—th—ship as big—a—nsport. Said it wa—eaded my—ay. Neutrons—on instruments—he's coming over the horizon—it's huge—war ship I think—register—instru—neutrons—." Abruptly the signals were blanked out completely.

Cole and Kendall sat frozen and stiff. Each looked at the other abruptly, then Kendall moved. From the receiver, he ripped out the recording coil, and instantly jammed it into the analyzer. He started it through once, then again, then again, at different tone settings, till he found a very shrill whine that seemed to clear up most of Nichols' bad key-work. "T-247—T-247—Emergency. Emergency. Randing reports the—over his horizon. Huge—ip—reign manufacture. Almost spherical. Randing's stopped. They got him I think. He said the ship was as big as a transport. Said it was headed my way. Neutrons—ont—gister—instruments. I think—is h—he's coming over the horizon. It's huge, and a war ship I think—register—instruments—neutrons."

Kendall's finger stabbed out at a button. Instantly the noise of the other men, wakened abruptly by the mild shocks, came from behind. Kendall swung to the controls, and Cole raced back to the engine room. The hundred-foot ship shot suddenly forward under the thrust of her tail ion-rockets. A blue-red cloud formed slowly behind her and expanded. Talbot appeared, and silently took her over from Kendall. "Stations, men," snapped Kendall. "Emergency call from a miner of Pluto reporting a large armed vessel which attacked them." Kendall swung back, and eased himself against the thrusting acceleration of the over-powered little ship, toward the engine room. Cole was bending over his apparatus, making careful check-ups, closing weapon-circuits. No window gave view of space here; on the left was the tiny tender's pocket, on the right, above and below the great water tanks that fed the ion-rockets, behind the rockets themselves. The tungsten metal walls were cold and gray under the ship lights; the hunched bulks of the apparatus crowded the tiny room. Gigantic racked accumulators huddled in the corners. Martin and Garnet swung into position in the fighting-tanks just ahead of the power rooms; Canning slid rapidly through the engine room, oozed through a tiny door, and took up his position in the stern-chamber, seated half-over the great ion-rocket sheath.

"Ready in positions, Captain Kendall," called the war-pilot as the little green lights appeared on his board.

"Test discharges on maximum," ordered Kendall. He turned to Cole. "You start the automatic key?"

"Right, Captain."

"All shipshape?"

"Right as can be. Accumulators at thirty-seven per cent, thanks to the loaf out here. They ought to pick up our signal back on Jupiter, he's nearest now. The station on Europa will get it."

"Talbot—we are only to investigate if the ship is as reported. Have you seen any signs of her?"

"No sir, and the signals are blank."

"I'll work from here." Kendall took his position at the commanding control. Cole made way for him, and moved to the power board. One by one he tested the automatic doors, the pressure bulkheads. Kendall watched the instruments as one after another of the weapons were tested on momentary full discharge—titanic flames of five million volt protons. Then the ship thudded to the chatter of the Garnell rifles.

Tensely the men watched the planet ahead, white, yet barely visible in the weak sunlight so far out. It was swimming slowly nearer as the tiny ship gathered speed.

Kendall cast a glance over his detector-instruments. The radio network was undisturbed, the magnetic and electric fields recognized only the slight disturbances occasioned by the planet itself. There was nothing, noth—

Five hundred miles away, a gigantic ship came into instantaneous being. Simultaneously, and instantaneously, the various detector systems howled their warnings. Kendall gasped as the thing appeared on his view screen, with the scale-lines below. The scale must be cock-eyed. They said the ship was fifteen hundred feet in diameter, and two thousand long!

"Retreat," ordered Kendall, "at maximum acceleration."

Talbot was already acting. The gyroscopes hummed in their castings, and the motors creaked. The T-247 spun on her axis, and abruptly the acceleration built up as the ion-rockets began to shudder. A faint smell of "heat" began to creep out of the converter. Immense "weight" built up, and pressed the men into their specially designed seats—

The gigantic ship across the way turned slowly, and seemed to stare at the T-247. Then it darted toward them at incredible speed till the poor little T-247 seemed to be standing still, as sailors say. The stranger was so gigantic now, the screens could not show all of him.

"God, Buck—he's going to take us!"

Simultaneously, the T-247 rolled, and from her broke every possible stream of destruction. The ion-rocket flames swirled abruptly toward her, the proton-guns whined their song of death in their housings, and the heavy pounding shudder of the Garnell guns racked the ship.

Strangely, Kendall suddenly noticed, there was a stillness in the ship. The guns and the rays were still going—but the little human sounds seemed abruptly gone.

"Talbot—Garnet—" Only silence answered him. Cole looked across at him in sudden white-faced amazement.

"They're gone—" gasped Cole.

Kendall stood paralyzed for thirty seconds. Then suddenly he seemed to come to life. "Neutrons! Neutrons—and water tanks! Old Nichols was right—" He turned to his friend. "Cole—the tender—quick." He darted a glance at the screen. The giant ship still lay alongside. A wash of ions was curling around her, splitting, and passing on. The pinprick explosions of the Garnell shells dotted space around her—but never on her.

Cole was already racing for the tender lock. In an instant Kendall piled in after him. The tiny ship, scarcely ten feet long, was powered for flights of only two hours acceleration, and had oxygen for but twenty-four hours for six men, seventy-two hours for two men—maybe. The heavy door was slammed shut behind them, as Cole seated himself at the panel. He depressed a lever, and a sudden smooth push shot them away from the T-247.

"DON'T!" called Kendall sharply as Cole reached for the ion-rocket control. "Douse those lights!" The ship was dark in dark space. The lighted hull of the T-247 drifted away from the little tender—further and further till the giant ship on the far side became visible.

"Not a light—not a sign of fields in operation." Kendall said, unconsciously speaking softly. "This thing is so tiny, that it may escape their observation in the fields of the T-247 and Pluto down there. It's our only hope."

"What happened? How in the name of the planets did they kill those men without a sound, without a flash, and without even warning us, or injuring us?"

"Neutrons—don't you see?"

"Frankly, I don't. I'm no scientist—merely a technician. Neutrons aren't used in any process I've run across."

"Well, remember they're uncharged, tiny things. Small as protons, but without electric field. The result is they pass right through an ordinary atom without being stopped unless they make a direct hit. Tungsten, while it has a beautifully high melting point, is mostly open space, and a neutron just sails right through it, or any heavy atom. Light atoms stop neutrons better—there's less open space in 'em. Hydrogen is best. Well—a man is made up mostly of light elements, and a man stops those neutrons—it isn't surprising it killed those other fellows invisibly, and without a sound."

"You mean they bathed that ship in neutrons?"

"Shot it full of 'em. Just like our proton guns, only sending neutrons."

"Well, why weren't we killed too?"

"'Water stops neutrons,' I said. Figure it out."

"The rocket-water tanks—all around us! Great masses of water—" gasped Cole. "That saved us?"

"Right. I wonder if they've spotted us."

The stranger ship was moving slowly in relation to the T-247. Suddenly the motion changed, the stranger spun—and a giant lock appeared in her side, opened. The T-247 began to move, floated more and more rapidly straight for the lock. Her various weapons had stopped operating now, the hoppers of the Garnell guns exhausted, the charge of the accumulators aboard the ship down so low the proton guns had died out.

"Lord—they're taking the whole ship!"

"Say—Cole, is that any ship you ever heard of before? I don't think that's just a pirate!"

"Not a pirate—what then?"

"How'd he get inside our detector screens so fast? Watch—he'll either leave, or come after us—" The T-247 had settled inside the lock now, and the great metal door closed after it. The whole patrol ship had been swallowed by a giant. Kendall was sketching swiftly on a notebook, watching the vast ship closely, putting down a record of its lines, and formation. He glanced up at it, and then down for a few more lines, and up at it—

The stranger ship abruptly dwindled. It dwindled with incredible speed, rushing off along the line of sight at an impossible velocity, and abruptly clicking out of sight, like an image on a movie-film that has been cut, and repaired after the scene that showed the final disappearance.

"Cole—Cole—did you get that? Did you see—do you understand what happened?" Kendall was excitedly shouting now.

"He missed us," Cole sighed. "It's a wonder—hanging out here in space, with the protector of the T-247's fields gone."

"No, no, you asteroid—that's not it. He went off faster than light itself!"

"Eh—what? Faster than light? That can't be done—"

"He did it, I know he did. That's how he got inside our screens. He came inside faster than the warning message could relay back the information. Didn't you see him accelerate to an impossible speed in an impossible time? Didn't you see how he just vanished as he exceeded the speed of light, and stopped reflecting it? That ship was no ship of this solar system!"

"Where did he come from then?"

"God only knows, but it's a long, long way off."

Chapter II

The IP-M-122 picked them up. The M-122 got out there two days later, in response to the calls the T-247 had sent out. As soon as she got within ten million miles of the little tender, she began getting Cole's signals, and within twelve hours had reached the tiny thing, located it, and picked it up.

Captain Jim Warren was in command, one of the old school commanders of the IP. He listened to Kendall's report, listened to Cole's tale—and radioed back a report of his own. Space pirates in a large ship had attacked the T-247, he said, and carried it away. He advised a close watch. On Pluto, his investigations disclosed nothing more than the fact that three mines had been raided, all platinum supplies taken, and the records and machinery removed.

The M-122 was a fifty-man patrol cruiser, and Warren felt sure he could handle the menace alone, and hung around for over two weeks looking for it. He saw nothing, and no further reports came of attack. Again and again, Kendall tried to convince him this ship he was hunting was no mere space pirate, and again and again Warren grunted, and went on his way. He would not send in any report Kendall made out, because to do so would add his endorsement to that report. He would not take Kendall back, though that was well within his authority.

In fact, it was a full month before Kendall again set foot on any of the Minor Planets, and then it was Mars, the base of the M-122. Kendall and Cole took passage immediately on an IP supply ship, and landed in New York six days later. At once, Kendall headed for Commander McLaurin's office. Buck Kendall, lieutenant of the IP, found he would have to make regular application to see McLaurin through a dozen intermediate officers.

By this time, Kendall was savagely determined to see McLaurin himself, and see him in the least possible time. Cole, too, was beginning to believe in Kendall's assertion of the stranger ship's extra-systemic origin. As yet neither could understand the strange actions of the machine, its attack on the Pluto mines, and the capture and theft of a patrol ship.

"There is," said Kendall angrily, "just one way to see McLaurin and see him quick. And, by God, I'm going to. Will you resign with me, Cole? I'll see him within a week then, I'll bet."

For a minute, Cole hesitated. Then he shook hands with his friends. "Today!" And that day it was. They resigned, together. Immediately, Buck Kendall got the machinery in motion for an interview, working now from the outside, pulling the strings with the weight of a hundred million dollar fortune. Even the IP officers had to pay a bit of attention when Bernard Kendall, multi-millionaire began talking and demanding things. Within a week, Kendall did see McLaurin.

At that time, McLaurin was fifty-three years old, his crisp hair still black as space, with scarcely a touch of the gray that appears in his more recent photographs. He stood six feet tall, a broad-shouldered, powerful man, his face grave with lines of intelligence and character. There was also a permanent narrowing of the eyes, from years under the blazing sun of space. But most of all, while those years in space had narrowed and set his eyes, they had not narrowed and set his mind. An infinitely finer character than old Jim Warren, his experience in space had taught him always to expect the unexpected, to understand the incomprehensible as being part of the unknown and incalculable properties of space and the worlds that swam in it. Besides the fine technical education he had started with, he had acquired a liberal education in mankind. When Buck Kendall, straight and powerful, came into his office with Cole, he recognized in him a character that would drive steadily and straight for its goal. Also, he recognized behind the millionaire that had succeeded in pulling wires enough to see him, the scientist who had had more than one paper published "in an amateur way."

"Dr. Bernard Kendall?" he asked, rising.

"Yes, sir. Late Buck Kendall, lieutenant of the IP. I quit and got Cole here to quit with me, so we could see you."

"Unusual tactics. I've had several men join up to get an interview with me." McLaurin smiled.

"Yes, I can imagine that, but we had to see you in a hurry. A hidebound old rapscallion by the name of Jim Warren picked us up out by Pluto, floating around in a six-man tender. We made some reports to him, but he wouldn't believe, and he wouldn't send them through—so we had to send ourselves through. Sir, this system is about to be attacked by some extra-systemic race. The IP-T-247 was so attacked, her crew killed off, and the ship itself carried away."

"I got the report Captain Jim Warren sent through, stating it was a gang of space pirates. Now what makes you believe otherwise?"

"That ship that attacked us, attacked with a neutron gun, a gun that shot neutrons through the hull of our ship as easily as protons pass through open space. Those neutrons killed off four of the crew, and spared us only because we happened to be behind the water tanks. Masses of hydrogen will stop neutrons, so we lived, and escaped in the tender. The little tender, lightless, escaped their observation, and we were picked up. Now, when the 247 had been picked up, and locked into their ship, that ship started accelerating. It accelerated so fast along my line of sight that it just dwindled, and—vanished. It didn't vanish in distance, it vanished because it exceeded the speed of light."

"Isn't that impossible?"

"Not at all. It can be done—if you can find some way of escaping from this space to do it. Now if you could cut across through a higher dimension, your projection in this dimension might easily exceed the speed of light. For instance, if I could cut directly through the Earth, at a speed of one thousand miles an hour, my projection on the surface would go twelve thousand miles while I was going eight. Similar, if you could cut through the four dimensional space instead of following its surface, you'd attain a speed greater than light."

"Might it not still be a space pirate? That's a lot easier to believe, even allowing your statement that he exceeded the speed of light."

"If you invented a neutron gun which could kill through tungsten walls without injuring anything within, a system of accelerating a ship that didn't affect the inhabitants of that ship, and a means of exceeding the speed of light, all within a few months of each other, would you become a pirate? I wouldn't, and I don't think any one else would. A pirate is a man who seeks adventure and relief from work. Given a means of exceeding the speed of light, I'd get all the adventure I wanted investigating other planets. If I didn't have a cent before, I'd have relief from work by selling it for a few hundred millions—and I'd sell it mighty easily too, for an invention like that is worth an incalculable sum. Tie to that the value of compensated acceleration, and no man's going to turn pirate. He can make more millions selling his inventions than he can make thousands turning pirate with them. So who'd turn pirate?"

"Right." McLaurin nodded. "I see your point. Now before I'd accept your statements in re the 'speed of light' thing, I'd want opinions from some IP physicists."

"Then let's have a conference, because something's got to be done soon. I don't know why we haven't heard further from that fellow."

"Privately—we have," McLaurin said in a slightly worried tone. "He was detected by the instruments of every IP observatory I suspect. We got the reports but didn't know what to make of them. They indicated so many funny things, they were sent in as accidental misreadings of the instruments. But since all the observatories reported them, similar misreadings, at about the same times, that is with variations of only a few hours, we thought something must have been up. The only thing was the phenomena were reported progressively from Pluto to Neptune, clear across the solar system, in a definite progression, but at a velocity of crossing that didn't tie in with any conceivable force. They crossed faster than the velocity of light. That ship must have spent about half an hour off each planet before passing on to the next. And, accepting your faster-than-light explanation, we can understand it."

"Then I think you have proof."

"If we have, what would you do about it?"

"Get to work on those 'misreadings' of the instruments for one thing, and for a second, and more important, line every IP ship with paraffin blocks six inches thick."

"Paraffin—why?"

"The easiest form of hydrogen to get. You can't use solid hydrogen, because that melts too easily. Water can be turned into steam too easily, and requires more work. Paraffin is a solid that's largely hydrogen. That's what they've always used on neutrons since they discovered them. Confine your paraffin between tungsten walls, and you'll stop the secondary protons as well as the neutrons."

"Hmmm—I suppose so. How about seeing those physicists?"

"I'd like to see them today, sir. The sooner you get started on this work, the better it will be for the IP."

"Having seen me, will you join up in the IP again?" asked McLaurin.

"No, sir, I don't think I will. I have another field you know, in which I may be more useful. Cole here's a better technician than fighter—and a darned good fighter, too—and I think that an inexperienced space-captain is a lot less useful than a second-rate physicist at work in a laboratory. If we hope to get anywhere, or for that matter, I suspect, stay anywhere, we'll have to do a lot of research pretty promptly."

"What's your explanation of that ship?"

"One of two things: an inventor of some other system trying out his latest toy, or an expedition sent out by a planetary government for exploration. I favor the latter for two reasons: that ship was big. No inventor would build a thing that size, requiring a crew of several hundred men to try out his invention. A government would build just about that if they wanted to send out an expedition. If it were an inventor, he'd be interested in meeting other people, to see what they had in the way of science, and probably he'd want to do it in a peaceable way. That fellow wasn't interested in peace, by any means. So I think it's a government ship, and an unfriendly government. They sent that ship out either for scientific research, for trade research and exploration, or for acquisitive exploration. If they were out for scientific research, they'd proceed as would the inventor, to establish friendly communication. If they were out for trade, the same would apply. If they were out for acquisitive exploration, they'd investigate the planets, the sun, the people, only to the extent of learning how best to overcome them. They'd want to get a sample of our people, and a sample of our weapons. They'd want samples of our machinery, our literature and our technology. That's exactly what that ship got.

"Somebody, somewhere out there in space, either doesn't like their home, or wants more home. They've been out looking for one. I'll bet they sent out hundreds of expeditions to thousands of nearby stars, gradually going further and further, seeking a planetary system. This is probably the one and only one they found. It's a good one too. It has planets at all temperatures, of all sizes. It is a fairly compact one, it has a stable sun that will last far longer than any race can hope to."

"Hmm—how can there be good and bad planetary systems?" asked McLaurin. "I'd never thought of that."

Kendall laughed. "Mighty easy. How'd you like to live on a planet of a Cepheid Variable? Pleasant situation, with the radiation flaring up and down. How'd you like to live on a planet of Antares? That blasted sun is so big, to have a comfortable planet you'd have to be at least ten billion miles out. Then if you had an interplanetary commerce, you'd have to struggle with orbits tens of billions of miles across instead of mere millions. Further, you'd have a sun so blasted big, it would take an impossible amount of energy to lift the ship up from one planet to another. If your trip was, say, twenty billions of miles to the next planet, you'd be fighting a gravity as bad as the solar gravity at Earth here all the way—no decline with a little distance like that."

"H-m-m-m—quite true. Then I should say that Mira would take the prize. It's a red giant, and it's an irregular variable. The sunlight there would be as unstable as the weather in New England. It's almost as big as Antares, and it won't hold still. Now that would make a bad planetary system."

"It would!" Kendall laughed. But as we know—he laughed too soon, and he shouldn't have used the conditional. He should have said, "It does!"

Chapter III

Gresth Gkae, Commander of Expeditionary Force 93, of the Planet Sthor, was returning homeward with joyful mind. In the lock of his great ship, lay the T-247. In her cargo holds lay various items of machinery, mining supplies, foods, and records. And in her log books lay the records of many readings on the nine larger planets of a highly satisfactory planetary system.

Gresth Gkae had spent no less than three ultra-wearing years going from one sun to another in a definitely mapped out section of space. He had investigated only eleven stars in that time, eleven stars, progressively further from the titanic red-flaming sun he knew as "the" sun. He knew it as "the" sun, and had several other appellations for it. Mira was so-named by Earthmen because it was indeed a "wonder" star, in Latin, mirare means "to wonder." Irregularly, and for no apparent reason it would change its rate of radiation. So far as those inhabitants of Sthor and her sister world Asthor knew, there was no reason. It just did it. Perhaps with malicious intent to be annoying. If so, it was exceptionally successful. Sthor and Asthor experienced, periodically, a young ice age. When Mira decided to take a rest, Sthor and Asthor froze up, from the poles most of the way to the equators. Then Mira would stretch herself a little, move about restlessly and Sthor and Asthor would become uninhabitably hot, anywhere within twenty degrees of the equator.

Those Sthorian people had evolved in a way that made the conditions endurable for savage or uncivilized people, but when a scientific civilization with a well-ordered mode of existence tried to establish itself, Mira was all sorts of a nuisance.

Gresth Gkae was a peculiar individual to human ways of thinking. He stood some seven feet tall, on his strange, double-knee'd legs and his four toed feet. His body was covered with little, short feather-like things that moved now with a volition of their own. They were moving very slowly and regularly. The space-ship was heated to a comfortable temperature, and the little fans were helping to cool Gresth Gkae. Had it been cold, every little feather would have lain down close against its neighbors, forming an admirable, wind-proof and cold-proof blanket.

Nature, on Sthor, had original ideas of arrangement too. Sthorians possessed two eyes—one directly above the other, in the center of their faces. The face was so long, and narrow, it resembled a blunt hatchet, with the two eyes on the edge. To counter-balance this vertical arrangement of the eyes, the nostrils had been separated some four inches, with one on each of the sloping cheeks. His ears were little pink-flesh cups on short, muscular stems. His mouth was narrow, and small, but armed with quite solid teeth adapted to his diet, a diet consisting of almost anything any creature had ever considered edible. Like most successful forms of intelligent life, Gresth Gkae was omnivorous. An intelligent form of life is necessarily adaptable, and adaptation meant being able to eat what was at hand.

One of his eyes, the upper one, was fully twice the size of the lower one. This was his telescopic eye. The lower, or microscopic eye was adapted to work for which a human being would have required a low power microscope, the upper eye possessed a more normal power of vision, plus considerable telescopic powers.

Gresth Gkae was using it now to look ahead in the blank of space to where gigantic Mira appeared. On his screens now, Mira appeared deep violet, for he was approaching at a speed greater than that of light, and even this projected light of Mira was badly distorted.

"The distance is half a light-year now, sir," reported the navigation officer.

"Reduce the speed, then, to normal velocity for these ranges. What reserve of fuel have we?"

"Less than one thousand pounds. We will barely be able to stop. We were too free in the use of our weapons, I fear," replied the Chief Technician.

"Well, what would you? We needed those things in our reports. Besides, we could extract fuel from that ore we took on at Planet Nine of Phahlo. It is merely that I wish speed in the return."

"As we all do. How soon do you believe the Council will proceed against the new system?"

"It will be fully a year, I fear. They must gather the expeditions together, and re-equip the ships. It will be a long time before all will have come in."

"Could they not send fast ships after them to recall them?"

"Could they have traced us as we wove our way from Thart to Karst to Raloork to Phahlo? It would be impossible."

Steadily the great ship had been boring on her way. Mira had been a disc for nearly two days, gigantic, two-hundred-and-fifty-million-mile Mira took a great deal of dwarfing by distance to lose her disc. Even at the Twin Planets, eight thousand two hundred and fifty millions of miles out, Mira covered half the sky, it seemed, red and angry. Sometimes, though, to the disgust of the Sthorians it was just red-faced and lazy. Then Sthor froze.

"Grih is in a descendant stage," said the navigation officer presently. "Sthor will be cold when we arrive."

"It will warm quickly enough with our news!" Gresth laughed. "A system—a delightful system—discovered. A system of many close-grouped planets. Why think—from one side of that system to the other is less of a distance than from Ansthat, our first planet's orbit, to Insthor's orbit! That sun, as we know, is steady and warm. All will be well, when we have eliminated that rather peculiar race. Odd, that they should, in some ways, be so nearly like us! Nearly Sthorian in build. I would not have expected it. Though they did have some amazing peculiarities! Imagine—two eyes just alike, and in a horizontal row. And that flat face. They looked as though they had suffered some accident that smashed the front of the face in. And also the peculiar beak-like projection. Why should a race ever develop so amazing a projection in so peculiar and exposed a position? It sticks out inviting attack and injury. Right in the middle of the face. And to make it worse, there is the air-channel, and the only air channel. Why, one minor injury to the throat would be certain to damage that passage beyond repair, and bring death. Yet such relatively unimportant things as ears, and eyes are doubled. Surely you would expect that so important a member as the air-passage would be doubled for safety.

"Those strange, awkward arms and legs were what puzzled me. I have been attempting to manipulate myself as they must be forced to, and I cannot see how delicate or accurate manual manipulation would be possible with those rigid, inflexible arms. In some ways I feel they must have had clever minds to overcome so great a handicap to constructive work. But I suppose single joints in the arms become as natural to them as our own more mobile two.

"I wonder if life in any intelligent form wouldn't develop somewhat similar formations, though. Think, in all parts of Sthor, before men became civilized and developed communication, even so much as twenty thousand years ago, our records show that seats and chairs were much as they are today, and much as they are, in all places among all groups. Then too, the eye has developed in many different species, and always reached much the same structure. When a thing is intended and developed to serve a given purpose, no matter who develops it, or where or how, is it not apt to have similar shapes and parts? A chair must have legs, and a seat and arm-rests and a back. You may vary their nature and their shape, but not widely, and they must be there. An eye must, anywhere, have a sensitive retina, an adjustable lens, and an adjustable device for controlling the entrance of light. Similarly there are certain functions that the body of an intelligent creature must serve which naturally tend to make intelligent creatures similar. He must have a tool—the hand—"

"Yes, yes—I see your point. It must be so, for surely these creatures out there are strange enough in other ways."

"But tell me, have you calculated when we shall land?"

"In twelve hours, thirty-three minutes, sir."

Eleven hours later, the expedition ship had slowed to a normal space-speed. On her left hung the giant globe of Asthor, rotating slowly, moving slowly in her orbit. Directly ahead, Sthor loomed even greater. Tiny Teelan, the thousand-mile diameter moon of the Insthor system shone dull red in the reflected light of gigantic Mira. Mira herself was gigantic, red and menacing across eight and a quarter billions of miles of space.

One hundred thousand miles apart, the twin worlds Sthor and Asthor rotated about their common center of gravity, eternally facing each other. Ten million miles from their common center of gravity, Teelan rotated in a vast orbit.

Sthor and Asthor were capped at each pole now by gigantic white icecaps. Mira was sulking, and as a consequence the planets were freezing.

The expedition ship sank slowly toward Sthor. A swarm of smaller craft had flown up at its approach to meet it. A gaily-colored small ship marked the official greeting-ship. Gresth had withheld his news purposely. Now suddenly he began broadcasting it from the powerful transmitter on his ship. As the words came through on a thousand sets, all the little ships began to whirl, dance and break out into glowing, sparkling lights. On Sthor and Asthor even commotions began to be visible. A new planetary system had been found— They could move! Their overflowing populations could be spread out!

The whole Insthor system went mad with delight as the great Expeditionary Ship settled downward.

Chapter IV

There was a glint of humor in Buck Kendall's eyes as he passed the sheet over to McLaurin. Commander McLaurin looked down the columns with twinkling eyes.

"'Petition to establish the Lunar Mining Bank,'" he read. "What a bank! Officers: President, General James Logan, late of the IP; Vice-president, Colonel Warren Gerardhi, also late of the IP; Staff, consists of 90% ex-IP men, and a few scattered accountants. Designed by the well-known designer of IP stations, Colonel Richard Murray." Commander McLaurin looked up at Kendall with a broad grin. "And you actually got Interplanetary Life to give you a mortgage on the structure?"

"Why not? It'll cut cost fifty-eight millions, with its twelve-foot tungsten-beryllium walls and the heavy defense weapons against those terrible pirates. You know we must defend our property."

"With the thing you're setting up out there on Luna, you could more readily wipe out the IP than anything else I know of. Any new defense ideas?"

"Plenty. Did you get any further appropriations from the IP Appropriations Board?"

McLaurin looked sour. "No. The dear taxpayers might object, and those thickheaded, clogged rockets on the Board can't see your data on the Stranger. They gave me just ten millions, and that only because you demonstrated you could shoot every living thing out of the latest IP cruiser with that neutron gun of yours. By the way, they may kick when I don't install more than a few of those."

"Let 'em. You can stall for a few months. You'll need that money more for other purposes. You've installed that paraffin lining?"

"Yes—I got a report on that of 'finished' last week. How have you made out?"

Buck Kendall's face fell. "Not so hot. Devin's been the biggest help—he did most of the work on that neutron gun really—"

"After," McLaurin interrupted, "you told him how."

"—but we're pretty well stuck now, it seems. You'll be off duty tomorrow evening, can't you drop around to the lab? We're going to try out a new system for releasing atomic energy."

"Isn't that a pretty faint hope? We've been trying to get it for three centuries now, and haven't yet. What chance at it within a year or so?—which is the time you allow yourself before the Stranger returns."

"It is, I'll admit that. But there's another factor, not to be forgotten. The data we got from correlating those 'misreadings' from the various IP posts mean a lot. We are working on an entirely different trail now. You come on out, and you can see our new apparatus. They are working on tremendous voltages, and hoping to smash the thing by a brutal bombardment of terrific voltage. We're trying, thanks to the results of those instruments, to get results with small, terrifically intense fields."

"How do you know that's their general system?"

"They left traces on the records of the post instruments. These records show such intensities as we never got. They have atomic energy, necessarily, and they might have had material energy, actual destruction of matter, but apparently, from the field readings it's the former. To be able to make those tremendous hops, light-years in length, they needed a real store of energy. They have accumulators, of course, but I don't think they could store enough power by the system they use to do it."

"Well, how's your trick 'bank' out on Luna, despite its twelve-foot walls, going to stand an atomic explosion?"

"More protective devices to come is our only hope. I'm working on three trails: atomic energy, some type of magnetic shield that will stop any moving material particle, and their faster-than-light thing. Also, that fortress—I mean, of course, bank—is going to have a lot of lead-lined rooms."

"I wish I could use the remaining money the Board gave me to lead-line a lot of those IP ships," said McLaurin wistfully. "Can't you make a gamma-ray bomb of some sort?"

"Not without their atomic energy release. With it, of course, it's easy to flood a region with rays. It'll be a million times worse than radium 'C,' which is bad enough."

"Well, I'll send through this petition for armaments. They'll pass it all right, I think. They may get some kicks from old Jacob Ezra Stubbs. Jacob Ezra doesn't believe in anything war-like. I wish they'd find some way to keep him off of the Arms Petition Board. He might just as well stay home and let 'em vote his ticket uniformly 'nay.'" Buck Kendall left with a laugh.

Buck Kendall had his troubles though. When he had reached Earth again, he found that his properties totaled one hundred and three million dollars, roughly. One doesn't sell properties of that magnitude, one borrows against them. But to all intents and purposes, Buck Kendall owned two half-completed ship's hulls in the Baldwin Spaceship Yards, a great deal of massive metal work on its way to Luna, and contracts for some very extensive work on a "bank." Beyond that, about eleven million was left.

A large portion of the money had been invested in a laboratory, the like of which the world had never seen. It was devoted exclusively to physics, and principally the physics of destruction. Dr. Paul Devin was the Director, Cole was in charge of the technical work, and Buck Kendall was free to do all the work he thought needed doing.

Returned to his laboratory, he looked sourly at the bench on which seven mechanicians were working. The ninth successive experiment on the release of atomic energy had failed. The tenth was in process of construction. A heavy pure tungsten dome, three feet in diameter, three inches thick, was being lowered over a clear insulum dome, a foot smaller. Inside, the real apparatus was arranged around the little pool of mercury. From it, two massive tungsten-copper alloy conductors led through the insulum housing, and outside. These, so Kendall had hoped, would surge with the power of broken atoms, but he was beginning to believe rather bitterly, they would never do so.

Buck went on to his offices, and the main calculator room. There were ten calculator tables here, two of them in operation now.

"Hello, Devin. Getting on?"

"No," said Devin bitterly, "I'm getting off. Look at these results." He brought over a sheaf of graphs, with explanatory tables attached. Rapidly Buck ran through them with him. Most of them were graphs of functions of light, considered as a wave in these experiments.

"H-m-m-m—not very encouraging. Looks like you've got the field—but it just snaps shut on itself and won't work. The lack of volume makes it break down, if you establish it, and makes it impossible to establish in the first place without the energy of matter. Not so hot. That's certainly cock-eyed somewhere."

"I'm not. The math may be."

"Well"—Kendall grinned—"it amounts to the same thing. The point is, light doesn't. Let's run over that theory again. Light is not only magnetic; but electric. Somehow it transforms electric fields cyclically into magnetic fields and back again. Now what we want to do is to transform an electric into a magnetic field and have it stay there. That's the first step. The second thing, is to have the lines of magnetic force you develop, lie down like a sheath around the ship, instead of standing out like the hairs on an angry cat, the way they want to. That means turning them ninety degrees, and turning an electric into a magnetic field means turning the space-strain ninety degrees. Light evidently forms a magnetic field whose lines of force reach along its direction of motion, so that's your starting point."

"Yes, and that," growled Devin, "seems to be the finishing point. Quite definitely and clearly, the graph looped down to zero. In other words, the field closed in on itself, and destroyed itself."

"Light doesn't vanish."

"I'll make you all the lights you want."

"I simply mean there must be something that will stop it."

"Certainly. Transform it back to electric field before it gets a chance to close in, then repeat the process—the way light does."

"That wouldn't make such a good magnetic shield. Every time that field started pulsing out through the walls of the ship it would generate heat. We want a permanent field that will stay on the job out there. I wonder if you couldn't make a conductor device that would open that field out—some special type of oscillating field that would keep it open."

"H-m-m-m—that's an angle I might try. Any suggestions?"

Kendall had suggestions, and rapidly he outlined a development that appeared from some of the earlier mathematics on light, and might be what they wanted.

Kendall, however, had problems of his own to work on. The question of atomic energy he was leaving alone, till the present experiment either succeeded, or, as he rather suspected, failed as had its predecessors. His present problem was to develop more fully some interesting lines of research he had run across in investigating mathematically the trick of turning electric to magnetic fields and then turning them back again. It might be that along this line he would find the answer to the speed greater than that of light. At any rate, he was interested.

He worked the rest of that day, and most of the next on that line—till he ran it into the ground with a pair of equations that ended with the expression: $dx.dv = h/(4\pi m)$. Then Kendall looked at them for a long moment, then he sighed gently and threw them into a file cabinet. Heisenberg's Uncertainty. He'd reduced the thing to a form that simply told him it was beyond the limits of certainty and he ran it into the normal, natural uncertainty inevitable in Nature.

Anyway he had real work to do now. The machine was about ready for his attention. The mechanicians had finished putting it in shape for demonstration and trial. He himself would have to test it over the rest of the afternoon and arrange for power and so forth.

By evening, when Commander McLaurin called around with some of the other investors in Kendall's "bank" on Luna, the thing was already started, warming up. The fields were being fed and the various scientists of the group were watching with interest. Power was flowing in already at a rate of nearly one hundred thousand horsepower per minute, thanks to a special line given them by New York Power (a Kendall property). At ten o'clock they were beginning to expect the reaction to start. By this time the fields weren't gaining in intensity very rapidly, a maximum intensity had been reached that should, they felt, break the atoms soon.

At eleven-thirty, through the little view window, Buck Kendall saw something that made him cry out in amazement. The mercury metal in the receiver, behind its layers of screening was beginning to glow, with a dull reddish light, and little solidifications were appearing in it! Eagerly the men looked, as the solidifications spread slowly, like crystals growing in an evaporating solution.

Twelve o'clock came and went, and one o'clock and two o'clock. Still the slow crystallization went on. Buck Kendall was casting furtive glances at the kilowatt-hour meter. It stood at a figure that represented twenty-seven thousand dollars' worth of power. Long since the power rate had been increased to the maximum available, as the power plant's normal load reduced as the morning hours came. Surely, this time something would start, but Buck had two worries. If all the enormous amount of energy they had poured in there decided to release itself at once—

And at any rate, Buck saw they'd never dare to let a generator stop, once it was started!

The men were a tense group around the machine at three-fifteen A.M. There remained only a tiny, dancing globule of silvery mercury skittering around on the sharp, needle-like crystals of the dull red metal that had resulted. Slowly that skittering drop was shrinking—

Three twenty-two and a half A.M. saw the last fraction of it vanish. Tensely the men stared into the machine—backing off slowly—watching the meters on the board. At nearly eighty thousand volts the power had been fed into it.

The power continued to flow, and a growing halo of intense violet light appeared suddenly on those red, needle-like crystals, a swiftly expanding halo—

Without a sound, without the slightest disturbance, the halo vanished, and softly, gently, the needle-like crystals relapsed, melted away, and a dull pool of metallic mercury rested in the receiver.

At eighty thousand volts, power was flowing in—

And it didn't even sparkle.

Chapter V

The apparatus of the magnetic shield had been completed two days later, and set up in Buck's own laboratory. On the bench was the powerful, but small, little projector of the straight magnetic field, simply a specially designed accumulator, a super-condenser, and the peculiar apparatus Devin had designed to distort the electric field through ninety degrees to a magnetic field. Behind this was a curious, paraboloid projector made up of hundreds of tiny, carefully orientated coils. This was Buck's own contribution. They were ready for the tests.

"I would invite McLaurin in to see this," said Kendall looking at them, and then across the room bitterly toward the alleged atomic power apparatus on the opposite bench. "I think it will work. But after that—" He stared, glaring, at the heavy tungsten dome with its heavy tungsten contacts, across which the flame of released atomic energy was supposed to have leapt. "That was probably the flattest flop any experiment ever flopped."

"Well—it didn't blow up. That's one comfort," suggested Devin.

"I wish it had. Then at least it would have shown some response. The only response shown, actually, was shown on the power meter. It damn near wore out the bearings turning so fast."

"Personally, I prefer the lack of action." Devin laughed. "Have you got that circuit hooked up?"

"Right," sighed Kendall, turning back to the work in hand. "Is Douglass in on this?"

"Yes—in the next room. He'll let us know when he's ready. He's setting up those instruments."

Douglass, a young junior physicist, late of the IP Physics Department, stuck his head in the door and announced his instruments were all set up.

"Keep an eye on them. They'll move somehow, at any rate. This thing couldn't go as flat as that atom-buster of mine."

Carefully Kendall made a few last-minute adjustments on the limiting relays, and took up his position at the power board. Devin took his place near the apparatus, with another series of instruments, similar to those Douglass was now watching in the next room, some thirty feet away, through the two-inch metal wall. "Ready," called Kendall.

The switch shot home. Instantly Kendall, Devin, and all the men in the building jumped some six feet from their former positions. A monstrous roar of sound crashed out in that laboratory that thundered from one wall to the other, and bellowed in a Titan's fury. It thundered and growled, it bellowed and howled, the walls shook with the march and counter-march of crashing waves of sound.

And a ten-foot wavering flame of blue-white, bellying electric fire shuddered up to the ceiling from the contact points of the alleged atomic generator. The heat, pouring out from the flashing, roaring arc sent prickles of aching burns over Kendall's skin. For ten seconds he stood in utter, paralyzed surprise as his flop of flops bellowed its anger at his disdain. Then he leapt to the power board and shut off the roaring thing, by cutting the switch that had started it.

"Spirits of Space! Did that come to life!"

"Atomic Energy!" Devin cried.

"Atomic energy, hell. That's my thirty thousand dollars' worth of power breaking loose again," chortled Kendall. "We missed the atomic energy, but, sweet boy, what an accumulator we stubbed our toes on! I wondered where in blazes all that power went to. That's the answer. I'll bet I can tell you right now what happened. We built that mercury up to a new level, and that transitional stage was the red, crystalline metal. When it reached the higher stage, it was temporarily stable—but that projector over there that we designed for the purpose of holding open electric and magnetic fields just opened the door and let all that power right out again."

"But why isn't it atomic energy? How do you know that no more than your power that you put in is coming out?" demanded Devin.

"The arc, man, the arc. That was a high-current, and low-voltage arc. Couldn't you tell by the sound that no great voltage—as atomic voltages go—was smashing across there? If we were getting atomic voltage—and power—there'd have been a different tone to it, high and shriller.

"Now, did you take any readings?"

"What do you think, man? I'm human. Do you think I got any readings with that thing bellowing and shrieking in my ears, and burning my skin with ultra-violet? It itches now."

Kendall laughed. "You know what to do for an itch. Now, I'm going to make a bet. We had those points separated for a half-million volts discharge, but there was a dust-cover thrown over them just now. That, you notice, is missing. I'll bet that served as a starter lead for the main arc. Now I'm going to start that projector thing again, and move the points there through about six inches, and that thing probably won't start itself."

Most of the laboratory staff had collected at the doorway, looking in at the white-hot tungsten discharge points, and the now silent "atomic engine." Kendall turned to them and said: "The flop picked itself up. You go on back, we seem to be all in one piece yet. Douglass, you didn't get any readings, did you?"

Sheepishly, Douglass grinned at him. "Eh—er—no—but I tore my pants. The magnetic field grabbed me and I jumped. They had some steel buttons, and a lot of steel keys—they're kinda' hard to keep on now."

The laboratory staff broke into a roar of laughter, as Douglass, holding up his trousers with both hands was beheld.

"I guess the field worked," he said.

"I guess maybe it did," adjudged Kendall solemnly. "We have some rope here if you need it—"

Douglass returned to his post.

Swiftly, Kendall altered the atomic distortion storage apparatus, and returned to the power-board. "Ready?"

"Check."

Kendall shoved home the switch. The storage device was silent. Only a slight feeling of strain made itself felt, and the sudden noisy hum of a small transformer nearby. "She works, Buck!" Devin called. "The readings check almost exactly."

"All good then. Now I want to get to that atomic thing. We can let that slide for a little bit—I'll answer it."

The telephone had rung noisily. "Kendall Labs—Kendall speaking."

"This is Superintendent Foster, of the New York Power, Mr. Kendall. We have some trouble just now that we think your operations may be responsible for. The sub-station at North Beaumont blew all the fuses, and threw the breakers at the main station. The men out there said the transformers began howling—"

"Right you are—I'm afraid I did do that. I had no idea that it would reach so far. How far is that from my place here?"

"It's about a thousand yards, according to the survey maps."

"Thanks—and I'll be careful about it. Any damage, I am responsible for? All okay?"

"Yes, sir, Mr. Kendall."

Kendall hung up. "We stirred up a lot more dust than we expected, Devin. Now let's start seeing if we can keep track of it. Douglass, how did your readings show?"

"I took them at the ten stations, and here they are. The stations are two feet apart."

"H-m-m—.5—.55—.6—.7—20—198—5950—6010—6012—5920. Very, very nice—only the darned thing's got an arm as long as the law. Your readings were about .2, Devin?"

"That's right."

"Then these little readings are just leakage. What's our normal intensity here?"

"About .19. Just a very small fraction less than the readings."

"Perfect—we have what amounts to a hollow shell of magnetic force—we can move inside, and you can move outside—far enough. But you can't get a conductor or a magnetic field through it." He put the readings on the bench, and looked at the apparatus across the room. "Now I want to start right on that other. Douglass, you move that magnetostat apparatus out of the way, and leave just the 'can-opener' of ours—the projector. I'm pretty sure that's what does the deed. Devin, see if you can hunt up some electrostatic voltmeters with a range in the neighborhood of—I think it'll be about eighty thousand."

Rapidly, Douglass was dismounting the apparatus, as Devin started for the stock room. Kendall started making some new connections, reconnecting the apparatus they had intended using on the "atomic engine," largely high-capacity resistances. He seemed to perform this work mechanically, his mind definitely on something else. Suddenly he stopped, and looked carefully into the receiver of the machine. The metal in it was silvery, liquid, and here and there a floating crystal of the dull red metal. Slowly a smile spread across his face. He turned to Douglass.

"Douglass—ah, you're through. Get on the trail of MacBride, and get him and his crew to work making half a dozen smaller things like this. Tell 'em they can leave off the tungsten shield. I want different metals i n t h e r e c e i v e r o f e a c h . Use—hmmm—sodium—copper—magnesium—aluminium, iron and chromium. Got it?"

"Yes, sir." He left, just as Devin returned with a large electrostatic voltmeter.

"I'd like," said he, "to know how you know the voltage will range around eighty thousand."

"K-ring excitation potential for mercury. I'm willing to bet that thing simply shoved the whole electron system of the mercury out a notch—that it simply hasn't any K-ring of electrons now. I'm trying some other metals. Douglass is going to have MacBride make up half a dozen more machines. Machines—they need a name. This—ah—this is an 'atostor.' MacBride's going to make up half a dozen of 'em, and try half a dozen metals. I'm almost certain that's not mercury in there now, at all. It's probably element 99 or something like it."

"It looks like mercury—"

"Certainly. So would 99. Following the periodic table, 99 would probably have an even lower melting point than mercury, be silvery, dense and heavy—and perhaps slightly radioactive. The series under the B family of Group II is Magnesium, Zinc, Cadmium, Mercury—and 99. The melting point is going down all the way, and they're all silvery metals. I'm going to try copper, and I fully expect it to turn silvery—in fact, to become silver."

"Then let's see." Swiftly they hooked up the apparatus, realigned the projector, and again Kendall took his place at the power-board. As he closed the switch, on no-load, the electrostatic voltmeter flopped over instantly, and steadied at just over 80,000 volts.

"I hate to say 'I told you so,'" said Kendall. "But let's hook in a load. Try it on about 100 amps first."

Devin began cutting in load. The resistors began heating up swiftly as more and more current flowed through them. By not so much as by a vibration of the voltmeter needle, did the apparatus betray any strain as the load mounted swiftly. 100—200—500—1000 amperes. Still, that needle held steady. Finally, with a drain of ten thousand amperes, all the equipment available could handle, the needle was steady as a rock, though the tremendous load of 800,000,000 watts was cut in and out. That, to atoms, atoms by the nonillions, was no appreciable load at all. There was no internal resistance whatever. The perfect accumulator had certainly been discovered.

"I'll have to call McLaurin—" Kendall hurried away with a broad, broad smile.

Chapter VI

"Hello, Tom?"

The telephone rattled in a peeved sort of way. "Yes, it is. What now? And when am I going to see you in a social sort of way again?"

"Not for a long, long time; I'm busy. I'm busy right now as a matter of fact. I'm calling up the vice-president of Faragaut Interplanetary Lines, and I want to place an order."

"Why bother me? We have clerks, you know, for that sort of thing," suggested Faragaut in a pained voice.

"Tom, do you know how much I'm worth now?"

"Not much," replied Faragaut promptly. "What of it? I hear, as a matter of fact that you're worth even less in a business way. They're talking quite a lot down this way about an alleged bank you're setting up on Luna. I hear it's got more protective devices, and armor than any IP station in the System, that you even had it designed by an IP designer, and have a gang of Colonels and Generals in charge. I also hear that you've succeeded in getting rid of money at about one million dollars a day—just slightly shy of that."

"You overestimate me, my friend. Much of that is merely contracted for. Actually it'll take me nearly nine months to get rid of it. And by that time I'll have more. Anyway, I think I have something like ten million left. And remember that way back in the twentieth century some old fellow beat my record. Armour, I think it was, lost a million dollars a day for a couple of months running.

"Anyway, what I called you up for was to say I'd like to order five hundred thousand tons of mercury, for delivery as soon as possible."

"What! Oh, say, I thought you were going in for business." Faragaut gave a slight laugh of relief.

"Tom, I am. I mean exactly what I say. I want five—hundred—thousand—tons of metallic mercury, and just as soon as you can get it."

"Man, there isn't that much in the system."

"I know it. Get all there is on the market for me, and contract to take all the 'Jupiter Heavy-Metals' can turn out. You send those orders through, and clean out the market completely. Somebody's about to pay for the work I've been doing, and boy, they're going to pay through the nose. After you've got that order launched, and don't make a christening party of the launching either, why just drop out here, and I'll show you why the value of mercury is going so high you won't be able to follow it in a space ship."

"The cost of that," said Faragaut, seriously now, "will be about—fifty-three million at the market price. You'd have to put up twenty-six cash, and I don't believe you've got it."

Buck laughed. "Tom, loan me a dozen million, will you? You send that order through, and then come see what I've got. I've got a break, too! Mercury's the best metal for this use—and it'll stop gamma rays too!"

"So it will—but for the love of the system, what of it?"

"Come and see—tonight. Will you send that order through?"

"I will, Buck. I hope you're right. Cash is tight now, and I'll probably have to put up nearer twenty million, when all that buying goes through. How long will it be tied up in that deal, do you think?"

"Not over three weeks. And I'll guarantee you three hundred percent—if you'll stay in with me after you start. Otherwise—I don't think making this money would be fair just now."

"I'll be out to see you in about two hours, Buck. Where are you? At the estate?" asked Faragaut seriously.

"In my lab out there. Thanks, Tom."

McLaurin was there when Tom Faragaut arrived. And General Logan, and Colonel Gerardhi. There was a restrained air of gratefulness about all of them that Tom Faragaut couldn't quite understand. He had been looking up Buck Kendall's famous bank, and more and more he had begun to wonder just what was up. The list of stockholders had read like a list of IP heroes and executives. The staff had been a list of

IP men with a slender sprinkling of accountants. And the sixty-million dollar structure was to be a bank without advertising of any sort! Usually such a venture is planned and published months in advance. This had sprung up suddenly, with a strange quietness.

Almost silently, Buck Kendall led the way to the laboratory. A small metal tank was supported in a peculiar piece of apparatus, and from it led a small platinum pipe to a domed apparatus made largely of insulum. A little pool of mercury, with small red crystals floating in it rested in a shallow hollow surrounded by heavy conductors.

"That's it, Tom. I wanted to show you first what we have, and why I wanted all that mercury. Within three weeks, every man, woman and child in the system will be clamoring for mercury metal. That's the perfect accumulator." Quickly he demonstrated the machine, charging it, and then discharging it. It was better than 99.95% efficient on the charge, and was 100% efficient on the discharge.

"Physically, any metal will do. Technically, mercury is best for a number of reasons. It's a liquid. I can, and do it in this, charge a certain quantity, and then move it up to the storage tank. Charge another pool, and move it up. In discharge, I can let a stream flow in continuously if I required a steady, terrific drain of power without interruption. If I wanted it for more normal service, I'd discharge a pool, drain it, refill the receiver, and discharge a second pool. Thus, mercury is the metal to use.

"Do you see why I wanted all that metal?"

"I do, Buck—Lord, I do," gasped Faragaut. "That is the perfect power supply."

"No, confound it, it isn't. It's a secondary source. It isn't primary. We're just as limited in the supply of power as ever—only we have increased our distribution of power. Lord knows, we're going to need a power supply badly enough before long—" Buck relapsed into moody silence.

"What," asked Faragaut, looking around him, "does that mean?"

It was McLaurin who told him of the stranger ship, and Kendall's interpretation of its meaning. Slowly Faragaut grasped the meaning behind Buck's strange actions of the past months.

"The Lunar Bank," he said slowly, half to himself. "Staffed by trained IP men, experts in expert destruction. Buck, you said something about the profits of this venture. What did you mean?"

Buck smiled. "We're going to stick up IP to the extent necessary to pay for that fort—er—bank—on Luna. We'll also boost the price so that we'll make enough to pay for those ships I'm having made. The public will pay for that."

"I see. And we aren't to stick the price too high, and just make money?"

"That's the general idea."

"The IP Appropriations Board won't give you what you need, Commander, for real improvements on the IP ships?"

"They won't believe Kendall. Therefore they won't."

"What did you mean about gamma rays, Buck?"

"Mercury will stop them and the Commander here intends to have the refitted ships built so that the engine room and control room are one, and completely surrounded by the mercury tanks. The men will be protected against the gamma rays."

"Won't the rays affect the power stored in the mercury—perhaps release it?"

"We tried it out, of course, and while we can't get the intensities we expect, and can't really make any measurements of the gamma-ray energy impinging on the mercury—it seems to absorb, and store that energy!"

"What's next on the program, Buck?"

"Finish those ships I have building. And I want to do some more development work. The Stranger will return within six months now, I believe. It will take all that time, and more for real refitting of the IP ships."

"How about more forts—or banks, whichever you want to call them. Mars isn't protected."

"Mars is abandoned," replied General Logan seriously. "We haven't any too much to protect old Earth, and she must come first. Mars will, of course, be protected as best the IP ships can. But—we're expecting defeat. This isn't a case of glorious victory. It will be a case of hard won survival. We don't know anything about the enemy—except that they are capable of interstellar flights, and have atomic energy. They are evidently far ahead of us. Our battle is to survive till we learn how to conquer. For a time, at least, the Strangers will have possession of most of the planets of the system. We do not think they will be able to reach Earth, because Commander McLaurin here will withdraw his ships to Earth to protect the planet—and the great 'Lunar Bank' will display its true character."

Chapter VII

Faragaut looked unsympathetically at Buck Kendall, as he stood glaring perplexedly at the apparatus he had been working on.

"What's the matter, Buck, won't she perk?"

"No, damn it, and it should."

"That," pointed out Faragaut, "is just what you think. Nature thinks otherwise. We generally have to abide by her opinions. What is it—or what is it meant to be?"

"Perfect reflector."

"Make a nice mirror. What else, and how come?"

"A mirror is just what I want. I want something that will reflect all the radiation that falls on it. No metal will, even in its range of maximum reflectivity. Aluminum goes pretty high, silver, on some ranges, a bit higher. But none of them reaches 99%. I want a perfect reflector that I can put behind a source of wild, radiant energy so I can focus it, and put it where it will do the most good."

"Ninety-nine percent. Sounds pretty good. That's better efficiency than most anything else we have, isn't it?"

"No, it isn't. The accumulator is 100% efficient on the discharge, and a good transformer, even before that, ran as high as 99.8 sometimes. They had to. If you have a transformer handling 1,000,000 horsepower, and it's even 1% inefficient, you have a heat loss of nearly 10,000 horsepower to handle. I want to use this as a destructive weapon, and if I hand the other fellow energy in distressing amounts, it's even worse at my end, because no matter how perfect a beam I work out, there will still be some spread. I can make it mighty tight though, if I make my surface a perfect parabola. But if I send a million horse, I have to handle it, and a ship can't stand several hundred thousand horsepower roaming around loose as heat, let alone the weapon itself. The thing will be worse to me than to him.

"I figured there was something worth investigating in those fields we developed on our magnetic shield work. They had to do, you know, with light, and radiant energy. There must be some reason why a metal reflects. Further, though we can't get down to the basic root of matter, the atom, yet, we can play around just about as we please with molecules and molecular forces. But it is molecular force that determines whether light and radiant energy of that caliber shall be reflected or transmitted. Take aluminum as an example. In the metallic molecule state, the metal will reflect pretty well. But volatilize it, and it becomes transparent. All gases are transparent, all metals reflective. Then the secret of perfect reflection lies at a molecular level in the organization of matter, and is within our reach. Well—this thing was supposed to make that piece of silver reflective. I missed it that time." He sighed. "I suppose I'll have to try again."

"I should think you'd use tungsten for that. If you do have a slight leak, that would handle the heat."

"No, it would hold it. Silver is a better conductor of heat. But the darned thing won't work."

"Your other scheme has." Faragaut laughed. "I came out principally for some signatures. IP wants one hundred thousand tons of mercury. I've sold most of mine already in the open market. You want to sell?"

"Certainly. And I told you my price."

"I know," sighed Faragaut. "It seems a shame though. Those IP board men would pay higher. And they're so damn tight it seems a crime not to make 'em pay up when they have to."

"The IP will need the money worse elsewhere. Where do I—oh, here?"

"Right. I'll be out again this evening. The regular group will be here?"

Kendall nodded as he signed in triplicate.

That evening, Buck had found the trouble in his apparatus, for as he well knew, the theory was right, only the practical apparatus needed changing. Before the group composed of Faragaut, McLaurin and the members of Kendall's "bank," he demonstrated it.

It was merely a small, model apparatus, with a mirror of space-strained silver that was an absolutely perfect reflector. The mirror had been ground out of a block of silver one foot deep, by four inches square, carefully annealed, and the work had all been done in a cooling bath. The result was a mirror that was so nearly a perfect paraboloid that the beam held sharp and absolutely tight for the half-mile range they tested it on. At the projector it was three and one-half inches in diameter. At the target, it was three and fifty-two one hundredths inches in diameter.

"Well, you've got the mirror, what are you going to reflect with it now?" asked McLaurin. "The greatest problem is getting a radiant source, isn't it? You can't get a temperature above about ten thousand degrees, and maintain it very long, can you?"

"Why not?" Kendall smiled.

"It'll volatilize and leave the scene of action, won't it?"

"What if it's a gaseous source already?"

"What? Just a gas-flame? That won't give you the point source you need. You're using just a spotlight here, with a Moregan Point-light. That won't give you energy, and if you use a gas-flame, the spread will be so great, that no matter how perfectly you figure your mirror, it won't beam."

"The answer is easy. Not an ordinary gas-flame—a very extra-special kind of gas-flame. Know anything about Renwright's ionization-work?"

"Renwright—he's an IP man isn't he?"

"Right. He's developed a system, which, thanks to the power we can get in that atostor, will sextuply ionize oxygen gas. Now: what does that mean?"

"Spirits of space! Concentrated essence of energy!"

"Right. And in preparation, Cole here had one made up for me. That—and something else. We'll just hook it up—"

With Devin's aid, Kendall attached the second apparatus, a larger device into which the silver block with its mirror surface fitted. With the uttermost care, the two physicists lined it up. Two projectors pointed toward each other at an angle, the base angles of a triangle, whose apex was the center of the mirror. On very low power, a soft, glowing violet light filtered out through the opening of the one, and a slight green light came from the other. But where the two streams met, an intense, violet glare built up. The center of action was not at the focus, and slowly this was lined up, till a sharp, violet beam of light reached out across the open yard to the target set up.

Buck Kendall cut off the power, and slowly got into position. "Now. Keep out from in front of that thing. Put on these glasses—and watch out." Heavy, thick-lensed orange-brown goggles were passed out, and Kendall took his place. Before him, a thick window of the same glass had been arranged, so that he might see uninterruptedly the controls at hand, and yet watch unblinded, the action of the beam.

Dully the mirror-force relay clicked. A hazy glow ran over the silver block, and died. Then—simultaneously the power was thrown from two small, compact atostors into the twin projectors. Instantly—a titanic eruption of light almost invisibly violet, spurted out in a solid, compact stream. With a roar and crash, it battered its way through the thick air, and crashed into the heavy target plate. A stream of flame and scintillating sparks erupted from the armor plate—and died as Kendall cut the beam. A white-hot area a foot across leaked down the face of the metal.

"That," said Faragaut gently, removing his goggles. "That's not a spotlight, and it's not exactly a gas-flame. But I still don't know what that blue-hot needle of destruction is. Just what do you call that tame stellar furnace of yours?"

"Not so far off, Tom," said Kendall happily, "except that even S Doradus is cold compared to that. That sends almost pure ultra-violet light—which, by the way, it is almost impossible to reflect successfully, and represents a temperature to be expressed not in thousands of degrees, nor yet in tens of thousands. I calculated the temperature would be about 750,000 degrees. What is happening is that a stream of low-voltage electrons—cathode rays—in great quantity are meeting great quantities of sextuply ionized oxygen. That means that a nucleus used to having two electrons in the K-ring, and six in the next, has had that outer six knocked off, and then has been hurled violently into free air.

"All by themselves, those sextuply ionized oxygen atoms would have a good bit to say, but they don't really begin to talk till they start roaring for those electrons I'm feeding them. At the meeting point, they grab up all they can get—probably about five—before the competition and the fierce release of energy drives them out, part-satisfied. I lose a little energy there, but not a real fraction. It's the howl they put up for the first four that counts. The electron-feed is necessary, because otherwise they'd smash on and ruin that mirror. They work practically in a perfect vacuum. That beam smashes the air out of the way. Of course, in space it would work better."

"How could it?" asked Faragaut, faintly.

"Kendall," asked McLaurin, "can we install that in the IP ships?"

"You can start." Kendall shrugged. "There isn't a lot of apparatus. I'm going to install them in my ships, and in the—bank. I suspect—we haven't a lot of time left."

"How near ready are those ships?"

"About. That's all I can say. They've been torn up a bit for installation of the atostor apparatus. Now they'll have to be changed again."

"Anything more coming?"

Buck smiled slowly. He turned directly to McLaurin and replied: "Yes—the Strangers. As to developments—I can't tell, naturally. But if they do, it will be something entirely unexpected now. You see, given one new discovery, a half-dozen will follow immediately from it. When we announced that atostor, look what happened. Renwright must have thought it was God's gift to suffering physicists. He stuck some oxygen in the thing, added some of his own stuff—and behold. The magnetic apparatus gave us directly the shield, and indirectly this mirror. Now, I seem to have reached the end for the time. I'm still trying to get that space-release for high speed—speed greater than light, that is. So far," he added bitterly, "all I've gotten as an answer is a single expression that simply means practical zero—Heisenberg's Uncertainty Expression."

"I'm uncertain as to your meaning"—McLaurin smiled—"but I take it that's nothing new."

"No. Nearly four centuries old—twentieth century physics. I'll have to try some other line of attack, I guess, but that did seem so darned right. It just sounded right. Something ought to happen—and it just keeps saying 'nothing more except the natural uncertainty of nature.'"

"Try it out, your math might be wrong somewhere."

Kendall laughed. "If it was—I'd hate to try it out. If it wasn't I'd have no reason to. And there's plenty of other work to do. For one thing, getting that apparatus in production. The IP board won't like me." Kendall smiled.

"They don't," replied McLaurin. "They're getting more and more and more worried—but they've got to keep the IP fleet in such condition that it can at least catch an up-to-date freighter."

Gresth Gkae looked back at Sthor rapidly dropping behind, and across at her sister world, Asthor, circling a bare 100,000 miles away. Behind his great interstellar cruiser came a long line of similar ships. Each was loaded now not with instruments and pure scientists, but with weapons, fuel and warriors. Colonists too, came in the last ships. One hundred and fifty giant ships. All the wealth of Sthor and Asthor had been concentrated in producing those great machines. Every one represented nearly the equivalent of thirty million Earth-dollars. Four and a half billions of dollars for mere materials.

Gresth Gkae had the honor of lead position, for he had discovered the planets and their stable, though tiny, sun. Still, Gresth Gkae knew his own giant Mira was a super-giant sun—and a curse and a menace to any rational society. Our yellow-white sun (to his eyes, an almost invisible color, similar to our blue) was small, but stable, and warm enough.

In half an hour, all the ships were in space, and at a given signal, at ten-second intervals, they sprang into the superspeed, faster than light. For an instant, giant Mira ran and seemed distorted, as though seen through a porthole covered with running water, then steadied, curiously distorted. Faster than light they raced across the galaxy.

Even in their super-fast ships, nearly three and a half weeks passed before the sun they sought, singled itself from the star-field as an extra bright point. Two days more, and the sun was within planetary distance. They came at an angle to the plane of the ecliptic, but they leveled down to it now, and slanted toward giant Jupiter and Jovian worlds. Ten worlds, in one sweep, it was—four habitable worlds. The nine satellites would be converted into forts at once, nine space-sweeping forts guarding the approaches to the planet. Gresth Gkae had made a fairly good search of the worlds, and knew that Earth was the main home of civilization in this system. Mars was second, and Venus third. But Jupiter offered the greatest possibilities for quick settlement, a base from which they could more easily operate, a base for fuels, for the heavy elements they would need—

Fifteen million miles from Jupiter they slowed below the speed of light—and the IP stations observed them. Instantly, according to instructions issued by Commander McLaurin, a fleet of ten of the tiniest, fastest scouts darted out. As soon as possible, a group of three heavy cruisers, armed with all the inventions that had been discovered, the atostor power system, perfectly conducting power leads, the terrible UV ray, started out.

The scouts got there first. Cameras were grinding steadily, with long range telescopic lenses, delicate instruments probed and felt and caught their fingers in the fields of the giant fleet.

At ten-second intervals, giant ships popped into being, and glided smoothly toward Jupiter.

Then the cruisers arrived. They halted at a respectful distance, and waited. The Miran ships plowed on undisturbed. Simultaneously, from the three leaders, terrific neutron rays shot out. The paraffin block walls stopped those—and the cruisers started to explain their feelings on the subject. They were the IP-J-37, 39, and 42. The 37 turned up the full power of the UV ray. The terrific beam of ultra-violet energy struck the second Miran ship, and the spot it touched exploded into incandescence, burned white-hot—and puffed out abruptly as the air pressure within blew the molten metal away.

The Mirans were startled. This was not the type of thing Gresth Gkae had warned them of. Gresth Gkae himself frowned as the sudden roar of the machines of his ship rose in the metal walls. A stream of ten-inch atomic bombs shrieked out of their tubes, fully glowing green things floated out more slowly, and immediately waxed brilliant. Gamma ray bombs—but they could be guarded against—

The three Solarian cruisers were washed in such frightful flame as they had never imagined. Streams of atomic bombs were exploding soundlessly, ineffectively in space, not thirty feet from them as they felt the sudden resistance of the magnetic shields. Hopefully, the 39 probed with her neutron gun. Nothing happened save that several gamma ray bombs went off explosively, and all the atomic bombs in its path exploded at once.

Gresth Gkae knew what that meant. Neutron beam guns. Then this race was more intelligent than he had believed. They had not had them before. Had he perhaps given them too much warning and information?

There was a sudden, deeper note in the thrumming roar of the great ship. Eagerly Gresth Gkae watched—and sighed in relief. The nearer of the three enemy ships was crumbling to dust. Now the other two were beginning to become blurred of outline. They were fleeing—but oh, so slowly. Easily the greater ship chased them down, till only floating dust, and a few small pieces of—

Gresth Gkae shrieked in pain, and horror. The destroyed ships had fought in dying. All space seemed to blossom out with a terrible light, a light that wrapped around them, and burned into him, and through him. His eyes were dark and burning lumps in his head, his flesh seemed crawling, stinging—he was being flayed alive—in shrieking agony he crumpled to the floor.

Hospital attachés came to him, and injected drugs. Slowly torturing consciousness left him. The doctors began working over his horribly burned body, shuddering inwardly as the protective, feather-like covering of his skin loosened, and dropped from his body. Tenderly they lowered him into a bath of chemicals—

"The terrible light which caused so much damage to our men," reported a physicist, "was analyzed, and found to have some extraordinary lines. It was largely mercury-vapor spectrum, but the spectrum of mercury-atoms in an impossibly strained condition. I would suggest that great care be used hereafter, and all men be equipped with protective masks when observations are needed. This sun is very rich in the infra-X-rays and ultra-visible light. The explosion of light, we witnessed, was dangerous in its consisting almost wholly of very short and hard infra-X-rays."

The physicist had a special term for what we know as ultra-violet light. To him, blue was ultra-violet, and exceedingly dangerous to red-sensitive eyes. To him, our ultra-violet was a long X-ray, and was designated by a special term. And to him—the explosion of the atostor reservoirs was a terrible and mystifying calamity.

To the men in the five tiny scout-ships, it was also a surprise, and a painful one. Even space-hardened humans were burned by the terrifically hard ultra-violet from the explosion. But they got some hint of what it had meant to the Mirans from the confusion that resulted in the fleet. Several of the nearer ships spun, twisted, and went erratically off their courses. All seemed uncontrolled momentarily.

The five scouts, following orders, darted instantly toward the Lunar Bank. Why, they did not know. But those were orders. They were to land there.

The reason was that, faster than any Solarian ship, radio signals had reached McLaurin, and he, and most of the staff of the IP service had been moved to the Lunar Bank. Buck Kendall had extended an invitation in this "unexpected emergency." It so happened that Buck Kendall's invitation got there before any description of the Strangers, or their actions had arrived. The staff was somewhat puzzled as to how this happened—

And now for the satellites of great Jupiter.

One hundred and fifty giant interstellar cruisers advanced on Callisto. They didn't pause to investigate the mines and scattered farms of the satellite, but ten great ships settled, and a horde of warriors began pouring out.

One hundred and forty ships reached Ganymede. One hundred and thirty sailed on. One hundred and thirty ships reached Europa—and they sailed on hurriedly, one hundred and twenty-nine of them. Gresth Gkae did not know it then, but the fleet had lost its first ship. The IP station on Europa had spoken back.

They sailed in, a mighty armada, and the first dropped through Europa's thin, frozen atmosphere. They spotted the dome of the station, and a neutron ray lashed out at it. On the other, undefended worlds, this had been effective. Here—it was answered by ten five-foot UV rays. Further, these men had learned something from the destruction of the cruisers, and ten torpedoes had been unloaded, reloaded with atostor mercury, and sent out bravely.

Easily the Mirans wiped out the first torpedo—

Shrieking, the Miran pilots clawed their way from the controls as the fearful flood of ultra-violet light struck their unaccustomed skins. Others too felt that burning flood.

The second torpedo they caught and deflected on a beam of alternating-current magnetism that repelled it. It did not come nearer than half a mile to the ship. The third they turned their deflecting beam on—and something went strangely wrong with the beam. It pulled that torpedo toward the ship with a sickening acceleration—and the torpedo exploded in that frightful violet flame.

Five-foot diameter UV beams are nothing to play with. The Mirans were dodging these now as they loosed atomic bombs, only to see them exploded harmlessly by neutron guns, or caught in the magnetic screen. Gamma ray bombs were as useless. Again the beam of disintegrating force was turned on—

The present opponent was not a ship. It was an IP defense station, equipped with everything Solarian science knew, and the dome was an eight-foot wall of tungsten-beryllium. The eight feet of solid, ultra-resistant alloy drank up that crumbling beam, and liked it. The wall did not fail. The men inside the fort jerked and quivered as the strange beam, a small, small fraction of it, penetrated the eight feet of outer wall, the six feet or so of intervening walls, and the mercury atostor reserves.

"Concentrate all those UV beams on one spot, and see if you can blast a hole in him before he shakes it loose," ordered the ray technician. "He'll wiggle if you start off with the beam. Train your sights on the nose of that first ship—when you're ready, call out."

"Ready—ready—" Ten men replied. "Fire!" roared the technician. Ten titanic swords of pure ultra-violet energy, energy that practically no unconditioned metal will reflect to more than fifty per cent, emerged. There was a single spot of intense incandescence for a single hundredth of a second—and then the energy was burning its way through the inner, thinner skins with such rapidity that they sputtered and flickered like a broken televisor.

One hundred and twenty-nine ships retreated hastily for conference, leaving a gutted, wrecked hull, broken by its fall, on Europa.

Triumphantly, the Europa IP station hurled out its radio message of the first encounter between a fort and the Miran forces.

Most important of all, it sent a great deal of badly wanted information regarding the Miran weapons. Particularly interesting was the fact that it had withstood the impact of that disintegrating ray.

Chapter VIII

Grimly Buck Kendall looked at the reports. McLaurin stood beside him, Devin sat across the table from him. "What do you make of it, Buck?" asked the Commander.

"That we have just one island of resistance left on the Jovian worlds. And that will, I fear, vanish. They haven't finished with their arsenal by any means."

"But what was it, man, what was it that ruined those ships?"

"Vibration. Somehow—Lord only knows how it's done—they can project electric fields. These projected fields are oscillated, and they are tuned in with some parts of the ship. I suspect they are crystals of the metals. If they can start a vibration in the crystals of the metal—that's fatigue, metal fatigue enormously speeded. You know how a quartz crystal oscillator in a radio-control apparatus will break, if you work it on a very heavy load at the peak? They simply smash the crystals of metal in the same way. Only they project their field."

"Then our toughest metals are useless? Can't something tough, rather than hard, like copper or even silver for instance, stand it?"

"Calcium metal's the toughest going—and even that would break under the beating those ships give it. The only way to withstand it is to have such a mass of metal that the oscillations are damped out. But—"

The set tuned in on the IP station on Europa was speaking again. "The ships are returning. There are one hundred and twenty-nine by accurate count. Jorgsen reports that telescopic observation of the dead on the fallen cruiser show them to be a completely un-human race! They are of mottled coloring, predominately grayish brown. The ships are returning. They have divided into ten groups, nine groups of two each, and a main body of the rest of the fleet. The group of eighteen is descending within range, and we are focusing our beams on them—"

Out by Europa, ten great UV beams were stabbing angrily toward ten great interstellar ships. The metal of the hulls glowed brilliant, and distorted slowly as the thick walls softened under the heat, and the air behind pressed against it. Grimly the ten ships came on. Torpedoes were being launched, and exploded, and now they had no effect, for the Mirans within were protected.

The eighteen grouped ships separated, and arranged themselves in a circle around the fort. Suddenly one staggered as a great puff of gas shot out through the thin atmosphere of Europa to flare brilliantly in the lash of the stabbing UV beam. Instantly the ship righted itself, and labored upward. Another dropped to take its place—

And the great walls of the IP fort suddenly groaned and started in their welded joints. The faint, whispering rustle of the crumbling beam was murmuring through the station. Engineers shouted suddenly as meters leapt the length of their scales, and the needles clicked softly on the stop pins. A thin rustle came from the atostors grouped in the great power room. "Spirits of Space—a revolving magnetic field!" roared the Chief Technician. "They're making this whole blasted station a squirrel cage!"

The mighty walls of eight-foot metal shuddered and trembled. The UV beams lashed out from the fort in quivering arcs now, they did not hold their aim steady, and the magnetic shield that protected them from atomic bombs was working and straining wildly. Eighteen great ships quivered and tugged outside there now, straining with all their power to remain in the same spot, as they passed on from one to another the magnetic impulses that were now creating a titanic magnetic vortex about the fort.

"The atostors will be exhausted in another fifteen minutes," the Chief Technician roared into his transmitter. "Can the signals get through those fields, Commander?"

"No, Mac. They've been stopped, Sparks tells me. We're here—and let's hope we stay. What's happening?"

"They've got a revolving magnetic field out there that would spin a minor planet. The whole blasted fort is acting like the squirrel cage in an induction motor! They've made us the armature in a five hundred million horsepower electric motor."

"They can't tear this place loose, can they?"

"I don't know—it was never—" The Chief stopped. Outside a terrific roar and crash had built up. White darts of flame leapt a thousand feet into the air, hurling terrific masses of shattered rock and soil.

"I was going to say," the Chief went on, "this place wasn't designed for that sort of a strain. Our own magnetic field is supporting us now, preventing their magnetic field from getting its teeth on metal. When the strain comes—well, they're cutting loose our foundation with atomic bombs!"

Five UV beams were combined on one interstellar ship. Instantly the great machine retreated, and another dropped in to take its place while the magnetic field spun on, uninterruptedly.

"Can they keep that up long?"

"God knows—but they have a hundred and more ships to send in when the power of one gives out, remember."

"What's our reserve now?"

The Chief paused a moment to look at the meters. "Half what it was ten minutes ago!"

Commander Wallace sent some other orders. Every torpedo tube of the station suddenly belched forth deadly, fifteen-foot torpedoes, most of them mud-torpedoes, torpedoes loaded with high explosive in the nose, a delayed fuse, and a load of soft clinging mud in the rear. The mud would flow down over the nose and offer a resistance foot-hold for the explosive which empty space would not. Four hundred and three torpedoes, equipped with anti-magnetic apparatus darted out. One hundred and four passed the struggling fields. One found lodgement on a Miran ship, and crushed in a metal wall, to be stopped by a bulkhead.

The Chief engineer watched his power declining. All ten UV beams were united in one now, driving a terrible sword of energy that made the attacked ship skip for safety instantly, yet the beams were all but useless. For the Miran reserves filled the gap, and the magnetic tornado continued.

For seventeen long minutes the station resisted the attack. Then the last of the strained mercury flowed into the receivers, and the vast power of the atostors was exhausted. Slowly the magnetic fields declined. The great walls of the station felt the clutching lines of force—they began to heat and to strain. A low, harsh grinding became audible over the roar of the atomic bombs. The whole structure trembled, and jumped slightly. The roar of bombs ceased suddenly, as the station jerked again, more violently. Then it turned a bit, rolled clumsily. Abruptly it began to spin violently, more and more rapidly. It started rolling clumsily across the plateau—

A rain of atomic bombs struck the unprotected metal, and the eighth breached the walls. The twentieth was the last. There was no longer an IP station on Europa.

"The difference," said Buck Kendall slowly, when the reports came in from scout-ships in space that had witnessed the last struggle, "between an atomic generator and an atomic power-store, or accumulator, is clearly shown. We haven't an adequate source of power."

McLaurin sighed slowly, and rose to his feet. "What can we do?"

"Thank our lucky stars that Faragaut here, and I, bought up all the mercury in the system, and had it brought to Earth. We at least have a supply of materials for the atostors."

"They don't seem to do much good."

"They're the best we've got. All the photocells on Earth and Venus and Mercury are at present busy storing the sun's power in atostors. I have two thousand tons of charged mercury in our tanks here in the 'Lunar Bank.'"

"Much good that will do—they can just pull and pull and pull till it's all gone. A starfish isn't strong, but he can open the strongest oyster just because he can pull from now on. You may have a lot of power—but."

"But—we also have those new fifteen-foot UV beams. And one fifteen-foot UV beam is worth, theoretically, nine five-foot beams, and practically, a dozen. We have a dozen of them. Remember, this place was designed not only to protect itself, but Earth, too."

"They can still pull, can't they?"

"They'll stop pulling when they get their fingers burned. In the meantime, why not use some of those IP ships to bring in a few more cargoes of charged mercury?"

"They aren't good for much else, are they? I wonder if those fellows have anything more we don't know?"

"Oh, probably. I'm going to work on that crumbler thing. That's the first consideration now."

"Why?"

"So we can move a ship. As it is, even those two we built aren't any good."

"Would they be anyway?"

"Well—I think I might disturb those gentlemen slightly. Remember, they each have a nose-beam eighteen feet across. Exceedingly unpleasant customers."

"Score: Strangers; magnetic field, atomic bombs, atomic power, crumbler ray. Home team; UV beams."

Kendall grinned. "I'd heard you were a pessimistic cuss when battle started—"

"Pessimistic, hell, I'm merely counting things up."

"McClellan had all the odds on Lee back in the Civil War of the States—but Lee sent him home faster than he came."

"But Lee lost in the end."

"Why bring that up? I've got work to do." Still smiling, Kendall went to the laboratory he had built up in the "Lunar Bank." Devin was already there, calculating. He looked unhappy.

"We can't do anything, as far as I can see. They're using an electric field all right, and projecting it. I can't see how we can do that."

"Neither can I," agreed Kendall, "so we can't use that weapon. I really didn't want to anyway. Like the neutron gun which I told Commander McLaurin would be useless as a weapon, they'd be prepared for it, you can be sure. All I want to do is fight it, and make their projection useless."

"Well, we have to know how they project it before we can break up the projection, don't we?"

"Not at all. They're using an electric field of very high frequency, but variable frequency. As far as I can see, all we need is a similar variable electric field of a slightly different frequency to heterodyne theirs into something quite harmless."

"Oh," said Devin. "We could, couldn't we? But how are you going to do that?"

"We'll have to learn, that's all."

Buck Kendall started trying to learn. In the meantime, the Mirans were taking over Jupiter. There were three IP stations on the planet itself, but they were vastly hindered by the thick, almost ultra-violet-proof atmosphere of Jupiter. Their rays were weak. And the magnetic fields of the Mirans were unaffected. Only their atomic bombs were hindered by the heavier gravity that pulled the rocks back in place faster than the bombs could throw them out. Still—a few hours of work, and the IP stations on Jupiter had rolled wildly across the flat plains of the planet like dented cans, to end in utter destruction.

The Mirans had paid no attention to the fleeing passenger and freighter ships that left the planet, loaded to the utmost with human cargo, and absolutely no freight. The IP fleet had to go to their rescue with oxygen tanks to take care of the extra humans, but nearly three-quarters of the population of Jupiter, a newly established population, and hence a readily mobile one, was saved. The others, the Mirans did not bother with particularly except when they happened to be near where the Mirans wanted to work. Then they were instantly destroyed by atomic bombing, or gamma rays.

The Mirans settled almost at once, and began their work of finding on Jupiter the badly needed atomic fuels. Machines were set up, and work begun, Mirans laboring under the gravity of the heavy planet. Then, fifty ships swam up again, reloaded with fuel, and with crews consisting solely of uninjured warriors, and started for Mars.

Mars was half way between her near conjunction and her maximum elongation with respect to Jupiter at that time. The Mirans knew their business though, for they started in on the IP station on Phobos. They were practiced by this time, and this IP station had only seven five-foot beams. In half an hour that station fell, and its sister station on Deimos followed. Three wounded ships returned to Jupiter, and ten new ships came out. The attack on Mars itself was started.

Mars was a different proposition. There were thirty-two IP stations here, one of them nearly as powerful as the Lunar Bank station. It was equipped with four of the huge fifteen-foot beams. And it had fifteen tons of mercury, more than seven-eighths charged. The Mars Center Station was located a short ten miles from the Mars Center City, and under the immediate orders of the IP heads, Mars Center City had been vacated.

For two days the Mirans hung off Mars, solidifying their positions on Phobos and Deimos. Then, with sixty-two ships, they attacked. They had made some very astute observations, and they started on the smaller stations just beyond the range of the Mars Center Station. Naturally, near so powerful a center, these stations had never been strong. They fell rapidly. But they had been counted on by Mars Center as auxiliary supports. McLaurin had sent very definite orders to Mars Center forbidding any action on their part, save gathering of power-supplies.

At last the direct attack on Mars Center was launched. For the first time, the Mirans saw one of the fifteen-foot beams. Mars' atmosphere is thin, and there is little ozone. The ultra-violet beams were nearly as effective as in empty space. When the Mirans dropped their ships, a full thirty of them, into the circle formation, Mars Center answered at once. All four beams started.

Those fifteen-foot beams, connected directly to huge atostor release apparatus, delivered a maximum power of two and three-quarter billion horsepower, each. The first Miran ship struck, sparkled magnificently, and a terrific cascade of white-hot metal rolled down from its nose. The great ship nosed down and to the left abruptly, accelerated swiftly—and crashed with tremendous energy on the plain outside of Mars Center City. White, unwavering flames licked up suddenly, and made a column five hundred feet high against the dark sky. Then the wreck exploded with a violence that left a crater half a mile across.

Three other ships had been struck, and were rapidly retreating. Another try was made for the ring formation, and four more ships were wounded, and replaced. The ring did not retreat, but the great magnetic field started. Atomic and gamma ray bombs started now, flashing sometimes dangerously close to the station as its magnetic field battled the rotating field of the ships. The four greater beams, and many smaller ones were in swift and angry action. Not more than a ten-second exposure could be endured by any one ship, before it must retreat.

For five minutes the Mirans hung doggedly at their task. Then, wisely, they retreated. Of the fleet, not more than seven ships remained untouched. Mars Center Station had held—at what cost only they knew. Five hundred tons of their mercury had been exhausted in that brief five minutes. One hundred tons a minute had flowed into and out of the atostor apparatus. Mars Center radioed for help, when the fleet lifted.

There was one other station on Mars that stood a good chance of survival, Deenmor Station, with three of the big beams installed, and apparatus for their fourth was in the station, and being rapidly worked over. McLaurin did a wise and courageous thing, at which every man on Mars cursed. He ordered that all IP stations save these two be deserted, and all mercury fuel reserves be moved to Deenmor and Mars Center.

The Mirans could not land on the North Western section of Mars, nor in the South Central region. Therefore Mars was not exactly habitable to Miran ships, because the great beams had been so perfectly figured that they were effective at a range of nearly twelve hundred miles.

Deenmor station was attacked—but it was a half-hearted attack, for Mirans were becoming distinctly skittish about fifteen-foot UV beams. Two badly blistered ships—and the Mirans retreated to Jupiter. But Mira held Phobos and Deimos. In two weeks, they had set up cannon there, and proved themselves accurate long-range gunners. Against the feeble attraction of Deimos, and with Mars' gravity to help them, they began bombarding the two stations, and anything that attempted to approach them, with gamma and atomic explosive bombs. Meanwhile they amused themselves occasionally by planting a gamma-ray bomb in each of Mars' major cities. They made Mars uninhabitable for Solarians as well as for Mirans, at least until the deadly slow-action atomic explosives wore off, or were removed.

Then the Mirans, after a lapse of three weeks while they dug in their toes on Jupiter, prepared to leap. Earth was the next goal. Miran scout-ships had been sent out before this—and severely handled by the concentrated fleets of the IP that hung grimly off Earth and Luna now. But the scouts had learned one thing. Mirans could never hope to attain a firm grasp on Earth while terribly armed Luna hung like a Sword of Damocles over their heads. Further, attack on Earth directly would be next to impossible, for, thanks to Faragaut's Interplanetary Company, nearly all the mercury metal in the system was safely lodged on Earth, and saturated with power. Every major city had been equipped with great UV apparatus. And neutron guns in plenty waited on small ships just outside the atmosphere to explode harmlessly any atomic or gamma bombs Miran ships might attempt to deposit.

An attack on Luna was the first step. But that terrible, gigantic fort on Luna worried them. Yet while that fort existed, Earth ships were free to come and go, for Mirans could not afford to stand near. At a distance of twenty thousand miles, small Miran ships had felt the touch of those great UV beams.

Finally, a brief test-attack was made, with an entire fleet of one hundred ships. They drew almost into position, faster than light, faster than the signaling warnings could send their messages. In position, all those great ships strained and heaved at the mighty magnetic vortex that twisted at the field of the fort. Instantly, twelve of the fifteen-foot UV beams replied. And—two great UV beams of a size the Mirans had never seen before, beams from the two ships, "S Doradus" and "Cepheid."

The test-attack dissolved as suddenly as it had come. The Mirans returned to Jupiter, and to the outer planets where they had further established themselves. Most of the Solar system was theirs. But the Solarians still held the choicest planets—and kept the Mirans from using the mild-temperatured Mars.

Chapter IX

"They can't take this, at least," sighed McLaurin as they retreated from Luna.

"I didn't think they could—right away. I'm wondering though if they haven't something we haven't seen yet. Besides which—give them time, give them time."

"Well, give us time, too," snapped McLaurin. "How are you coming?"

Buck smiled. "I'm sure I don't know. I have a machine but I haven't the slightest idea of whether or not it's any good."

"Why not?"

"I can destroy—I hope—but I can't build up their ray. I can't test the machine because I haven't their ray to test it against."

"What can we do to test it?"

"The only thing I can see is to call for volunteers—and send out a six-man cruiser. If the ship's too small, they may not destroy it with the big crumbler rays. If it's too large—and the machine didn't work—we'd lose too much."

Twelve hours later, the IP men at the Lunar Bank fort were lined up. McLaurin stepped up on the platform, and addressed the men briefly, told them what was needed. Six volunteers were selected by a process of elimination, those who were married, had dependents, officers, and others were refused. Finally, six men of the IP were chosen, neither rookies nor veterans, six average men. And one average six-man cruiser, one hundred and eleven feet long, twenty-two in diameter. It was the T-208, a sister ship of the T-247, the first ship to be destroyed.

The T-208 started out from Luna, and with full acceleration, sped out toward Phobos. Slowly she circled the satellite, while distant scouts kept her under view. Lazily, the Miran patrol on Phobos watched the T-208, indifferent to her. The T-208 dove suddenly, after five fruitless circles of the tiny world, and with her four-foot UV beam flaming, stabbed angrily at a flight of Miran scouts berthed in the very shadow of a great battle cruiser, one of the interstellar ships stationed here on Phobos.

Four of the little ships slumped in incandescence. Angrily the terrific sword of energy slashed at the frail little scouts.

Angrily the Miran interstellar ship shot herself abruptly into action against this insolent cruiser. The cruiser launched a flight of the mercury-torpedoes. Flashing, burning, ultra-violet energy flooded the great ship, harmlessly, for the men were, as usual, protected. The Miran answered with the neutron beam, atomic and gamma bombs—and the crumbler ray.

Gently, softly a halo of shimmering-violet luminescence built up about the T-208. The UV beam continued to flare, wavering slightly in its aim—then fell way off to one side. The T-208 staggered suddenly, wandered from her course—whole, but uncontrolled. For the men within the ship were dead.

Majestically the Miran swung along beside the dead ship, a great magnetic tow-cable shot out toward it, to shy off at first, then slowly to be adjusted, and take hold in the magnetic shield of the T-208. The pilots of the watching scout-ships turned away. They knew what would happen.

It did. Five—ten—twenty seconds passed. Then the "dead-man" took over the ship—and the stored power in the atostor tanks blasted in a terrible flame that shattered the metal hull to molecular fragments. The interstellar cruiser shuddered, and rolled half over at the blasting pressure. Leaking seams appeared in her plates.

The scouts raced back to Luna as the Miran settled heavily, and a trifle clumsily to Phobos. Miran radio-beams were forcing their way out toward the Miran station on Europa, to be relayed to the headquarters on Jupiter, just as Solarian radio beams were thrusting through space toward Luna. Said the Miran messages: "Their ships no longer crumble." Said the Solarian messages: "The ships no longer crumble—but the men die."

His deep eyes burning tensely, Buck Kendall heard the messages coming in, and rose slowly from his seat to pace the floor. "I think I know why," he said at last. "I should have thought. For that too can be prevented."

"Why—what in the name of the Planets?" asked McLaurin. "It didn't kill the men in the forts—why does it kill the men in the ships, when the ships are protected?"

"The protection kills them."

"But—but they had the protective oscillations on all the way out!" protested the Commander.

"Think how it works though. Think, man. The enemy's field is an electric-field oscillation. We combat it by setting up a similar oscillating field in the metal of the hull ourselves. Because the metal conducts the strains, they meet, and oppose. It is not a shield—a shield is impossible, as I have said, because of energy concentration factors. If their beam carried a hundred thousand horsepower in a ten-foot square beam, in every ten square feet of our shield, we'd have to have one hundred thousand horsepower. In other words, hundreds of times as much energy would be needed in the shield, as they used in their beam. We can't afford that. We had to let the beams oppose our oscillations in the metal, where, because the metal conducts, they meet on an equal basis. But—when two oscillations of slightly different frequency meet, what is the result?"

"In this case, a heterodyne frequency of a lower, and harmless frequency."

"So I thought. I was partly right. It does not harm the metal. But it kills the men. It is super-sonic. The terrible, shrill sounds destroy the cells of the men's bodies. Then, when their dead hands release the controls, the automatic switches blow up the ship."

"God! We stop one menace—and it is like the Hydra. For every head we lop off, two spring up."

"Ah—but they are lesser heads. Look, what is the fundamental difference between sound and light?"

"One is a vibration of matter and the—ah—eliminate the material contact!"

"Exactly! All we need to do is to let the ships operate airless, the men in space suits. Then the air cannot carry the sounds to them. And by putting special damping materials in their suits, we can stop the vibrations that would reach them through their feet and hands. Another six-man ship must go out—but this ship will come back!"

And with the order for another experimental ship, went the orders for commercial supplies of this new apparatus. Every IP ship must be equipped to resist it.

Buck Kendall sailed on the six-man scout that went out this time. Again they swooped once at Phobos, again Miran scout-ships crumbled under the attack of the vicious UV beams. The Mirans were not waiting contemptuously this time. In an instant the great interstellar ship rose from its berth, its weapons working angrily. The crumbler ray snapped out at the T-253.

Kendall stared into the periscope visor intently. Clumsily his padded hands worked at the specially adapted controls. The soft hiss of the oxygen release into his suit disturbed him slightly. The radio-phones in his helmet carried all the conversations in the ship to him with equal clarity. He watched as the great ship angled angrily up—

His vision was momentarily obscured by a violet glow that built up and reached out gently from every point of metal in the ship. The instant Kendall saw that, the T-253 was fleeing under his hands. The test had been made. Now all he desired was safety again. The ion-rockets flared recklessly as, crushed under an acceleration of four Earth-gravities, he sank heavily into his seat. Grimly the Miran ship was pursuing them, easily keeping up with the fleeing midget. The crumbler became more intense, the violet glow more vivid.

The UV beam was reaching out directly behind now. The—

With a cry of agony, Kendall ripped the radio-phone connection out of his suit. A soft hiss of leaking air warned him of too great violence only minutes later. For his ears had been deafened by the sudden shriek of a tremendous signal from outside!

Instantly Kendall knew what that meant. And he could not communicate with his men! There was no metal in these special suits, even the oxygen tanks were made of synthetic plastics of tremendous strength. No scrap of vibrating metal was permissible. The padded gloves and boots protected him—but there was a new and different type of crackle and haze from the metal points now. It was almost invisible in the practically airless ship, but Kendall saw it.

Presently he felt it, as he desperately increased his acceleration. Slow creeping heat was attacking him. The heat was increasing rapidly now. Desperately he was working at the crumbler-protection controls—but immediately set them back as they were. He had to have the crumbler protection as well—!

Grimly the great Miran ship hung right beside them. Angrily the two four-foot UV beams flashed back—seeking some weak spot. There were none. At her absolute maximum of acceleration the little ship plunged on. Gamma and atomic bombs were washing her in flame. The heavy blocks of paraffin between her walls were long since melted, retained only by the presence of the metal walls. Smoke was beginning to filter out now, and Kendall recognized a new, and deadlier menace! Heat—quantities of heat were being poured into the little ship, and the neutron guns were doing their best to add to it. The paraffin was confined in there—and like any substance, it could be volatilized, and as a vapor, develop pressure—explosive pressure!

The Miran seemed satisfied in his tactics so far—and changed them. Forty-seven million miles from Earth, the Miran simply accelerated a bit more, and crowded the Solarian ship a bit. White-faced, Buck Kendall was forced to turn a bit aside. The Miran turned also. Kendall turned a bit more—

Flashing across his range of vision at an incredible speed, a tiny thing, no more than twenty feet long and five in diameter, a scout-ship appeared. Its tiny nose ultra-violet beam was blasting a solid cylinder of violet incandescence a foot across in the hull of the Miran—and, to the Miran, angling swiftly across his range of vision. Its magnetic field clashed for a thousandth of a second with the T-253, instantly meeting, and absorbing the fringing edges. Then—it swept through the Miran's magnetic shield as easily. The delicate instruments of the scout instantaneously adjusted its own magnetic field as much as possible. There was resistance, enormous resistance—the ship crumpled in on itself, the tail vanished in dust as a sweeping crumbler beam caught it at last—and the remaining portion of the ship plowed into the nose of the Miran.

The Miran's force-control-room was wrecked. For perhaps a minute and a half, the ship was without control, then the control was re-established—and in vain the telescopes and instruments searched for the T-253. Lightless, her rockets out now, her fields damped down to extinction, the T-253 was lost in the pulsing, gyrating fields of half a dozen scout-ships.

Kendall looked grimly at the crushed spot on the nose of the Miran. His ship was drifting slowly away from the greater ship. Presently, however, the Miran put on speed in the direction of Earth, and the T-253 fell far behind. The Miran was not seriously injured. But that scout pilot, in sacrificing life, had thrown dust in their eyes for just those few moments Kendall had needed to lose a lightless ship in lightless space—lightless—for the Mirans at any rate. The IP ships had been covered with a black paint, and in no time at all, Kendall had gotten his ship into a position where the energy radiations of the sun made him undetectable from the Miran's position, since the radiation of his own ship, even in the heat range, was mingled with the direct radiation of the sun. The sun was in the Miran's "eyes," both actual and instrumental.

An hour later the Miran returned, passed the still-lightless ship at a distance of five million miles, and settled to Phobos for the slight repairs needed.

Twelve hours later, the T-253 settled to Luna, for the many rearrangements she would need.

"I rather knew it was coming," Kendall admitted sadly, "but danged if I didn't forget all about it. And—cost the life of one of the finest men in the system. Jehnson's family get a permanent pension just twice his salary, McLaurin. In the meantime—"

"What was it? Pure heat, but how?"

"Pure radio. Nothing but short-wave radio directed at us. They probably had the apparatus, knew how to make it, but that's not a good type of heat ray, because a radio tube is generally less than eighty percent efficient, which is a whale of a loss when you're working in a battle, and a whale of an inconvenience. We were heated only four times as much as the Miran. He had to pump that heat into a heat-reservoir—a water tank probably—to protect himself. Highly inefficient and ineffective against a large ship. Also, he had to hold his beam on us nearly ten minutes before it would have become unbearable. He was again, trying to kill the men, and not the ship. The men are the weakest point, obviously."

"Can you overcome that?"

"Obviously, no. The thing works on pure energy. I'd have to match his energy to neutralize it. You knew it's an old proposition, that if you could take a beam of pure, monochromatic light and divide it exactly in half, and then recombine it in perfect interference, you'd have annihilation of energy. Cancellation to extinction. The trouble is, you never do get that. You can't get monochromatic light, because light can't be monochromatic. That's due to the Heisenberg Uncertainty—my pet bug-bear. The atom that radiates the light, must be moving. If it isn't, the emission of the light itself gives it a kick that moves it. Now, no matter what the quantum might have been, it loses energy in kicking the atom. That changes the situation instantly, and incidentally the 'color' of the light. Then, since all the radiating atoms won't be moving alike, etc., the mass of light can't be monochromatic. Therefore perfect interference is impossible.

"The way that relates to the problem in hand, is that we can't possibly destroy his energy. We can, as we do in the crumbler stunt, change it. He can't, I suspect, put too much power behind his crumbler, or he'd have crumbling going on at home. We get a slight heating from it, anyway. Into the bargain, his radio was after us, and his neutrons naturally carried energy. Now, no matter what we do, we've got that to handle. When we fight his crumbler, we actually add heat-energy to it, ourselves, and make the heating effect just twice as bad. If we try to heterodyne his radio—presto—it has twice the heat energy anyway, though we might reduce it to a frequency that penetrated the ship instead of all staying in it. But by the proposition, we have to use as much energy, and in fact, remember the 80% rule. We've got to take it and like it."

"But," objected McLaurin, "we don't like it."

"Then build ships as big as his, and he'll quit trying to roast you. Particularly if the inner walls are synthetic plastics. Did you know I used them in the 'S Doradus' and 'Cepheid'?"

"Yes. Were you thinking of that?"

"No—just luck—and the fact that they're light, strong as steel almost, and can be manufactured in forms much more quickly. Only the outer hull is tungsten-beryllium. The advantage in this will be that nearly all the energy will be absorbed outside, and we'll radiate pretty fast, particularly as that tungsten-beryllium has a high radiation-factor in the long heat range."

"What does that mean?"

"Well, ordinary polished silver is a mighty poor radiator. Homely example: Try waiting for your coffee to cool if it's in a polished silver pot. Then try it in a tungsten-beryllium pot. No matter how you polish that tungsten-beryllium, the stuff WILL radiate heat. That's why an IP ship is always so blamed cold. You know the passenger ships use polished aluminum outer walls. The big help is, that the tungsten-beryllium will throw off the energy pretty fast, and in a big ship, with a whale of a lot of matter to heat, the Strangers will simply give up the idea."

"Yes, but only two ships in the system compare with them in size."

"Sorry—but I didn't build the IP fleet, and there are lots of tungsten and beryllium on Earth. Enough anyway."

"Will they use that beam on the fort? And can't we use the thing on them?"

"They won't and we won't—though we could. A bank of those new million watt tubes—perhaps a hundred of them—and we'd have a pretty effective heater—but an awful waste of power. I've got something better."

"New?"

"Somewhat. I've found out how to make the mirror field in a plate of metal, instead of a block. Come on to the lab, and I'll show you."

"What's the advantage? Oh—weight saved, and silver metal saved."

"A lot more than that, Mac. Watch."

At the laboratory, the new apparatus looked immensely lighter and simpler than the old. The atostor, the ionizer, and the twin ion-projectors were as before, great, rigid, metal structures that would maintain the meeting point of the ions with inflexible exactitude under any acceleration strains. But now, instead of the heavy silver block in which a mirror was figured, the mirror consisted of a polished silver plate, parabolic to be sure, but little more than a half-inch in thickness. It was mounted in a framework of complex, stout metal braces.

Kendall started the ion-flame at low intensity, so the UV beam was little more than a spotlight.

"You missed the point, Mac. Now—watch that tungsten-beryllium plate. I'll hold the power steady. It's an eighteen-inch beam—and now the energy is just sufficient to heat that tungsten plate to bright red. But—"

Kendall turned over a small rheostat control—and abruptly the eighteen-inch diameter spot on the tungsten-beryllium plate began contracting; it contracted till it was a blazing, sparkling spot of molten incandescence less than an inch across!

"That's the advantage of focus. At this distance of a few hundred feet with a small beam I can do that. With a twenty-foot beam, I can get a two-foot spot at a distance of nearly ten miles! That means that the receiving end will have the pleasure of handling one hundred times the energy concentration. That would punch a hole through most anything. All you have to do is focus it. The trouble being, if it's out of focus the advantage is more than lost. So if there's any question about getting the focus, we'll get along without it."

"A real help, if you do. That would punch a hole before the Stranger ship could turn away as they do now."

Kendall nodded. "That's what I was after. It is mainly for the forts, though. We'll have to signal the dope to the Mars Center and Deenmor stations. They can fix it up, themselves. In the meantime—all we can do is hold on and hunt, and let's hope better than the Strangers do."

Chapter X

Sadly the convalescent Gresth Gkae listened to the reports of his lieutenants. More and more disgraced he felt as he realized how badly he had blundered in reporting the people of this system unable to cope with the attackers' weapons. Gresth Gkae looked up at his old friend and physician, Merth Skahl. He shook his head slowly. "I'm afraid, Merth Skahl. I am afraid. We have, perhaps, made a mistake. The better and the stronger alone should rule. Aye, but is the stronger always the better? I am afraid we have mistaken the Truth in assuming this. If we have—then may Jarth, Lord of Truth and Wisdom punish us. Mighty Jarth, if I have mistaken in following my judgments, it is not from disobedience, it is lack of Thy knowledge. The strongest—they are not always the better, are they?"

Merth Skahl bent sharply over his friend. "Quiet thyself, Gresth Gkae. You know, and I know, you have done only your best, and surely Jarth himself can ask no better of any one. You must rest, for only by rest can those terrible burns be healed. All your stheen over half the body-area was burned off. You have been delirious for many days."

"But Merth Skahl, think—have we disobeyed Jarth's will? It is, we know, his will that only the best and the strongest shall rule—but are the best always the strongest? An imbecile adult could destroy the life of a genius-grade child. The strongest wins, but not the best. Such would not be the will of Jarth. If we be the stronger, and the best, then it is right and just that these strange creatures should be destroyed that we may have a stable world of stable light and heat. But look and see, with what terrible swiftness these strange creatures have learned! May it not be they are the better race—that it is we who are the weaker and the poorer? Can it be that Jarth has brought us together that these people might learn—and destroy us? If they be the stronger, and the better—then may Jarth's will be done. But we must test our strength to the utmost. I must rise, and go to my laboratory soon. They have set it up?"

"Aye, they have, Gresth Gkae. But remember, the weak and the sick make faults the strong and the well do not. Better that you rest yourself. There is little you can do while your body seeks to recover from these terrible burns."

"You are wrong, my friend, wrong. Don't you see that my mind is clear—that it is the mind which must fight in these battles, for surely the man is weak against such things as this infra-X-radiation? Why, I am better able to fight now than are you, for I am a trained fighter of the mind, while you are a trained healer of the body. These strange beings with their stiff arms and legs, their tender skins, and—and their swift minds have fought us all too well. If we must test, let it be a test. I have heard how they so quickly solved the riddle of the crumbling field. That took us longer, and we designed it. The Counsel of Worlds put me in command, let me up, Skahl, I must work."

Concerned, the physician looked down at him. Finally he spoke again. "No, I will not permit you to leave the hospital-ship. You must stay here, but if, as you have said, the mind is what must fight, then surely you can fight well from here, for your mind is here."

"No, I cannot, and you well know it. I may shorten my life, but what matter. 'Death is the end toward which the chemical reaction, Life, tends,'" quoted the scientist. "You know I have left my children—my immortality is assured through them. I can afford to die in peace, if it assures their welfare. Time is precious, and while my mind might work from here, it must have data on which to work. For that, I must go to the laboratories. Help me, Merth Skahl."

Reluctantly the physician granted the request, but begged of Gresth Gkae a promise of at least six hours rest in every fifteen, and a good sleep of at least twenty-seven hours every "night." Gresth Gkae agreed, and from a wheelchair, conducted his work, began a new line of experimentation he hoped would yield them the weapon they needed. Under him, the staff of scientists worked, aiding and advising and suggesting. The apparatus was built, tested, and found wanting. Time and again as the days passed, they watched Gresth Gkae, gaining strength very, very slowly, taken away despondent at the end of his forty hours of work.

A dozen expeditions were sent to Jupiter's poles to watch and measure and study the tremendous auroral displays there, where Jupiter's vast magnetic field sucked in countless quintillions of the flying electrons from the sun, and brought them circling in, in a vast, magnificent display of auroral ionization.

Expeditions went to the great Southern Plateau, the Plateau of Storms, where the titanic air currents resulted in an everlasting display of terrific lightnings, great burning balls of electric force floating dangerous and deadly across the frozen, ultra-cold plain.

And the expeditions brought back data. Yet still Gresth Gkae could not sleep, his thoughts intruding constantly. Hours Merth Skahl spent with him, calming him to sleep.

"But what is this constant search? It is little enough I know of science, but why do you send our men to these spots of wonderfully beautiful, but useless natural forces. Can we somehow, do you think, turn them against the people of these worlds?"

Softly the old Miran smiled. "Yes, you might say so. For look, it is the strange balls of electric force I want to know about. Sthor had few, but occasionally we saw them. Never were they properly investigated. I want to know their secret, for I am sure they are balls of electric forces not vastly dissimilar from the nucleus of the atom. Always we have known that no system of purely electrical forces could remain stable. Yet these strange balls of energy do. How is it? I am sure it will be of vast importance. But the direct secret I hope to learn is in this: What can be done with electric fields can nearly always be duplicated, or paralleled in magnetic fields. If I can learn how to make these electric balls of energy, can I not hope to make similar magnetic balls of energy?"

"Yes, I see—that would seem true. But what benefit would you derive from that? You have magnetic beams now, and yet they are useless because you can get nowhere near the forts. How then would these benefit you?"

"We can do nothing to those forts, because of that magnetic shield. Could we once break it down, then the fort is helpless, and one or two small atomic bombs destroy it. But—we cannot stay near, for the terrible infra-X-rays of theirs burn holes in our ships, and—in our men.

"But look you, I can drop many atomic bombs from a distance where their beams are ineffective. Suppose I do make a magnetic ball of energy, a magnetic bomb. Then—I can drop it from a distance! We have learned that the power supply of these forts is very great—but not endless, as is ours now, thanks to the vast supplies of power metal on this heavy planet. Then all we need do is stay at a distance where they cannot reach us—and drop magnetic bombs. Ah, they will be stopped, and their energy absorbed. But we can keep it up, day after day, and slowly drain out their power. Then—then our atomic bombs can destroy those forts, and we can move on!" But suddenly the animation and strength left his voice. He turned a sad, downcast face to his friend. "But Merth Skahl, we can't do it," he complained.

"Ah—now I can see why you so want to continue this wearing and worrying work. You need time, Gresth Gkae, only time for success. Tomorrow it may be that you will see the first hint that will lead you to success."

"Ah—I only hope it, Merth Skahl, I only hope it."

But it was the next day that they saw the first glimpse of the secret, and saw the path that might lead to hope and success. In a week they were sending electric bombs across the laboratory. And in three days more, a magnetic bomb streaked dully across the laboratory to a magnetic shield they had set up, and buried itself in it, to explode in brilliant light and heat.

From that day Gresth Gkae began to mend. In the three weeks that were needed to build the apparatus into ships, he regained strength so that when the first flight of five interstellar ships rose from Jupiter, he was on the flagship.

To Phobos they went first, to the little inner satellite of Mars, scarcely eight miles in diameter, a tiny bit of broken metal and rock, utterly airless, but scarcely more than 3700 miles from the surface of Mars below. The Mars Center and Deenmor forts were wasting no power raying a ship at that distance. They could, of course, have damaged it, but not severely enough to make up for the loss of their strictly limited power. The photocells had been working overtime, every minute of available light had been used, and still scarcely 2100 tons of charged mercury remained in the tanks of Mars Center and 1950 in the tanks at Deenmor.

The flight of five ships settled comfortably upon Phobos, while the three relieved of duty started back to Jupiter. Immediately work was begun on the attack. The ships were first landed on the near side, while the apparatus of the projectors was unloaded, then the great ships moved around to the far side. Phobos of course rotated with one face fixed irrevocably toward Mars itself, the other always to the cold of space. Great power leads trailed beneath the ships, and to the dark side. Then there were huge water lines for cooling. On this almost weightless world, where the great ships weighing hundreds of thousands of tons on a planet, weighed so little they were frequently moved about by a single man, the laying of five miles of water conduit was no impossibility.

Then they were ready. Mars Center came first. Automatic devices kept the aim exact, as the first of the magnetic bombs started down. At five-second intervals they were projected outward, invisible globes of concentrated magnetic energy, undetectable in space. Seven seconds passed before the first became dimly visible in the thin air of Mars. It floated down, it would miss the fort it seemed—so far to one side— Abruptly it turned, and darted with tremendously accelerating speed for the great magnetic field of the fort. With a vast blast of light, it exploded. Five seconds later a second exploded. And a third.

Mars Center signaled scoffingly that the bombs were all being stopped dead in the magnetic atmosphere, after the bombardment had been witnessed from Earth and Luna. An hour later they gave a report that they were concentrated magnetic fields of energy that would be rather dangerous—if it weren't that they couldn't even stand into the magnetic atmosphere. Three hours later Mars Center reported that they contained considerably more energy than had at first been thought. Further, which they had not carefully considered at first, they were taking energy with them! They were taking away about an equal amount of energy as each blew up.

It was only a half-hour after that that the men at Mars Center realized perfectly what it meant. Their power was being drained just a little bit better than twice as fast as they generated during the day—and since Phobos spun so swiftly across the sky.

Deenmor got the attack just about the time Mars Center was released. Deenmor immediately began seeking for the source of it. Somewhere on Phobos—but where?

The Mirans were experts at camouflage. Deenmor Station, realizing the menace, immediately rayed the "projector." They tore up a great deal of harmless rock with their huge UV rays. But the bomb device continued to throw one bomb each five seconds.

When Deenmor operated from Phobos' position, Mars Center was exposed to the deadly, constant drain. A day or two later, the bombs were coming one each second and a half, for more ships had joined in the work on Phobos.

Gresth Gkae saw the work was going nicely. He knew that now it was only a question of time before those magnetic shields would fail—and then the whole fort would be powerless. Maybe—it might be a good idea, when the forts were powerless to investigate instead of blowing them up. There might be many interesting and worthwhile pieces of apparatus—particularly the UV beam's apparatus.

Chapter XI

Buck Kendall entered the Communications room rather furtively. He hated the place. Cole was there, and McLaurin. Mac was looking tired and drawn, Cole not so tired, but equally drawn. The signals were coming through fairly well, because most of the disturbance was rising where the signals rose, and all the disturbance, practically, was magnetic rather than electric.

"Deenmor is sending, Buck," McLaurin said as he entered. "They're down to the last fifty-five tons. They'll have more time now—a rest while Phobos sinks. Mars Center has another 250 tons, but—it's just a question of time. Have you any hope to offer?"

"No," said Kendall in a strained voice. "But, Mac, I don't think men like those are afraid to die. It's dying uselessly they fear. Tell 'em—tell 'em they've defended not alone Mars, but all the system, in holding up the Strangers on Mars. We here on Luna have been safer because of them. And tell—Mac, tell them that in the meantime, while they defended us, and gave us time to work, we have begun to see the trail that will lead to victory."

"You have!" gasped McLaurin.

"No—but they will never know!" Kendall left hastily. He went and stood moodily looking at the calculator machines—the calculator machines that refused to give the answers he sought. No matter how he might modify that original idea of his, no matter what different line of attack he might try in solving the problems of Space and Matter, while he used the system he knew was right—the answer came down to that deadly, hope-blasting expression that meant only "uncertain."

Even Buck was beginning to feel uncertain under that constant crushing of hope. Uncertainty—uncertainty was eating into him, and destroying—

From the Communications room came the hum and drive of the great sender flashing its message across seventy-two millions of miles of nothing. "B-u-c-k K-e-n-d-a-l-l s-a-y-s h-e h-a-s l-e-a-r-n-e-d s-o-m-e-t-h-i-n-g t-h-a-t w-i-l-l l-e-a-d t-o v-i-c-t-o-r-y w-h-i-l-e y-o-u h-e-l-d b-a-c-k t-h-e—"

Kendall switched on a noisy, humming fan viciously. The too-intelligible signals were drowned in its sound.

"And—tell them to—destroy the apparatus before the last of the power is gone," McLaurin ordered softly.

The men in Deenmor station did slightly better than that. Gradually they cut down their magnetic shield, and some of the magnetic bombs tore and twisted viciously at the heavy metal walls. The thin atmosphere of Mars leaked in. Grimly the men waited. Atomic bombs—or ships to investigate? It did not matter much to them personally—

Gresth Gkae smiled with his old vigor as he ordered one of the great interstellar ships to land beside the powerless station, approaching from such an angle that the still-active Mars Center station could not attack. One of the fleet of Phobos rose, and circled about the planet, and settled gracefully beside the station. For half an hour it lay there quietly, waiting and watching. Then a crew of two dozen Mirans started across the dry, crumbly powder of Mars' sands, toward the fort. Simultaneously almost, three things happened. A three-foot UV beam wiped out the advancing party. A pair of fifteen-foot beams cut a great gaping hole in the wall of the interstellar ship, as it darted up, like a startled quail, its weapons roaring defiance, only to fall back, severely wounded.

And the radio messages pounded out to Earth the first description of the Miran people. Methodically the men in Deenmor station used all but one ton of their power to completely and forever wreck and destroy the interstellar cripple that floundered for a few moments on the sands a bare mile away. Presently, before Deenmor was through with it, the atomic bombs stopped coming, and the atomic shells. The magnetic shield that had been re-established for the few minutes of this last, dying sting, fell.

Deenmor station vanished in a sudden, colossal tongue of blue-green light as the ton of atomically distorted mercury was exploded by a projector beam turned on the tank.

It was long gone, when the first atomic bombs and magnetic bombs dropped from Phobos reached the spot, and only hot rock and broken metal remained.

Mars Center failed in fact the next time Phobos rode high over it. The apparatus here had been carefully destroyed by technicians with a view of making it indecipherable, but the Mirans made it even more certain, for no ship settled here to investigate, but a stream of atomic bombs that lasted for over an hour, and churned the rock to dust, and the dust to molten lava, in which pools of fused tungsten-beryllium alloy bubbled slowly and sank.

"Ah, Jarth—they are a brave race, whatever we may say of their queer shape," sighed Gresth Gkae as the last of Mars Center sank in bubbling lava. "They stung as they died." For some minutes he was silent.

"We must move on," he said at length. "I have been thinking, and it seems best that a few ships land here, and establish a fort, while some twenty move on to the satellite of the third planet and destroy the fort there. We cannot operate against the planet while that hangs above us."

Seven ships settled to Mars, while the fleet came up from Jupiter to join with Gresth Gkae's flight of ships on its way to Luna.

An automatically controlled ship was sent ahead, and began the bombardment. It approached slowly, and was not destroyed by the UV beams till it had come to within 40,000 miles of the fort. At 60,000 Gresth Gkae stationed his fleet—and returned to 150,000 immediately as the titanic UV beams of the Lunar Fort stretched out to their maximum range. The focus made a difference. One ship started limping back to Jupiter, in tow of a second, while the rest began the slow, methodical work of wearing down the defenses of the Lunar Fort.

Kendall looked out at the magnificent display of clashing, warring energies, the great, whirling spheres and discs of opalescent flame, and turned away sadly. "The men at Deenmor must have watched that for days. And at Mars Center."

"How long can we hold out?" asked McLaurin.

"Three weeks or so, at the present rate. That's a long time, really. And we can escape if we want to. The UV beams here have a greater range than any weapon the Strangers have, and with Earth so near—oh, we could escape. Little good."

"What are you going to do?"

"I," said Buck Kendall, suddenly savage, "am going to consign all the math machines in the universe to eternal damnation—and go ahead and build a machine anyway. I know that thing ought to be right. The math's wrong."

"There is no other thing to try?"

"A billion others. I don't know how many others. We ought to get atomic energy somehow. But that thing infuriates me. A hundred things that math has predicted, that I have checked by experiment, simple little things. But—when I carry it through to the point where I can get something useful—it wriggles off into—uncertainty."

Kendall stalked off to the laboratory. Devin was there working over the calculus machines, and Kendall called him angrily. Then more apologetic, he explained it was anger at himself. "Devin, I'm going to make that thing, if it blows up and kills me. I'm going to make that thing if this whole fort blows up and kills me. That math has blown up in my face for four solid months, and half killed me, so I'm going to kill it. Come on, we'll make that damned junk."

Angrily, furiously, Kendall drove his helpers to the task. He had worked out the apparatus in plan a dozen times, and now he had the plans turned into patterns, the patterns into metal.

Saucily, the "S Doradus" made the trip to and from Earth with patterns, and with metal, with supplies and with apparatus. But she had to dodge and fight every inch of the way as the Miran ships swooped down angrily at her. A fighting craft could get through when the Miran fleet was withdrawn to some distance, but the Mirans were careful that no heavy-loaded freighter bearing power supply should get through.

And Gresth Gkae waited off Luna in his great ship, and watched the steady streams of magnetic bombs exploding on the magnetic shield of the Lunar Fort. Presently more ships came up, and added their power to the attack, for here, the photo-cell banks could gather tremendous energy, and Gresth Gkae knew he would need to overcome this, and drain the accumulated power.

Gresth Gkae felt certain if he could once crack this nut, break down Earth, he would have the system. This was the home planet. If this fell, then the two others would follow easily, despite the fact that the few forts on the innermost planet, Mercury, could gather energy from the sun at a rate greater than their ships could generate.

It took Kendall two weeks and three days to set up his preliminary apparatus. They had power for perhaps four days more, thanks to the fact that the long Lunar day had begun shortly after Gresth Gkae's impatient attack had started. Also, the "S Doradus" had brought in several hundred tons of charged mercury on each trip, though this was no great quantity individually, it had mounted up in the ten trips she had made. The "Cepheid," her sister ship, had gone along on seven of the trips, and added to the total.

But at length the apparatus was set up. It was peculiar looking, and it employed a great deal of power, nearly as much as a UV beam in fact. McLaurin looked at it sceptically toward the last, and asked Buck: "What do you expect it to do?"

"I am," said Kendall sourly, "uncertain. The result will be uncertainty itself."

Which, considering things, was a surprisingly accurate statement. Kendall gave the exact answer. He meant to give an ironic comment. For the mathematics had been perfectly correct, only Buck Kendall misinterpreted the answer.

"I've followed the math with mechanism all the way through," he explained, "and I'm putting power into it. That's all I know. Somewhere, by the laws of cause and effect, this power must show itself again—despite what the damn math says."

And in that, of course, Kendall was wrong. Because the laws of cause and effect didn't hold in what he was doing now.

"Do you want to watch?" he asked at length. "I'm all set to try it."

"I suppose I may as well." McLaurin smiled. "In our close-knit little community the fate of one is of interest to all. If it's going to blow up, I might as well be here, and if it isn't, I want to be."

Kendall smiled appreciatively and replied: "Let it be on thy own head. Here she goes."

He walked over to the power board, and took command. Devin, and a squad of other scientists were seated about the room with every conceivable type and combination of apparatus. Kendall wanted to see what this was doing. "Tubes," he called. "Circuits A and D. Tie-ins." He stopped, the preliminary switches in. "Main circuit coming." With a jerk he threw over the last contact. A heavy relay thudded solidly. The hum of a straining atostor. Then—

An electric motor, humming smoothly stopped with a jerk. "This," it remarked in a deep throaty voice, "is probably the last stand of humanity."

The galvanometer before which Devin was seated apparently agreed. In a rather high pitched voice it pointed out that: "If the Lunar Fort falls, the Earth—" It stopped abruptly, and an electroscope beside Douglass took up the thread in a high, shrill voice, rather slurred, "—will be directly attacked."

"This," resumed the motor in a hoarse voice, "will certainly mean the end of humanity." The motor gave up the discourse and hummed violently into action—in reverse!

"My God!" Kendall pulled the switch open with a sagging jaw and staring eyes.

The men in the room burst into sudden startled exclamations.

Kendall didn't give them time. His jaw snapped shut, and a blazing light of wondrous joy shone in his eyes. He instantly threw the switch in again. Again the humming atostor, the strain—

Slowly Devin lifted from his seat. With thrashing arms and startled, staring eyes, he drifted gently across the room. Abruptly he fell to the floor, unhurt by the light Lunar gravity.

"I advise," said the motor in its grumbling voice, "an immediate exodus." It stopped speaking, and practiced what it preached. It was a fifty-horse motor-generator, on a five-ton tungsten-beryllium base, but it rose abruptly, spun rapidly about an axis at right angles to the axis of its armature, and stopped as suddenly. In mid air it continued its interrupted lecture. "Mercury therefore is the destination I would advise. There power is sufficient for—all machines." Gently it inverted itself and settled to the middle of the floor. Kendall instantly cut the switch. The relay did not chunk open. It refused to obey. Settled in the middle of the floor now, torn loose from its power leads, the motor-generator began turning. It turned faster and faster. It was shrilling in a thin scream of terrific speed, a speed that should have torn its windings to fragments under the lash of centrifugal force. Contentedly it said throatily. "Settled."

The galvanometer spoke again in its peculiar harsh voice. "Therefore, move." Abruptly, without apparent reason, the stubborn relay clicked open. The shrilly screaming motor stopped dead instantly, as though it had had no real momentum, or had been inertialess.

Startled, white-faced men looked at Kendall. Buck's eyes were shining with an unholy glee.

"Uncertainty!" he shouted. "Uncertainty—uncertainty—uncertainty, you fools! Don't you see it? All the math—it said uncertainty—man, man—we've got just that—uncertainty!"

"You're crazy," gasped McLaurin. "I'm crazy, everything's gone crazy."

Kendall roared with sudden, joyous laughter. "Absolutely. Everything goes crazy—the laws of nature break down! Heisenberg's principle showed that the law of cause and effect weren't absolute. We've made them absolutely uncertain!"

"But—but motors talking, instruments giving lectures—"

"Certainly—or rather uncertainly—anything, absolutely anything. The destruction of the laws of gravity, freedom from inertia—why, merely picking up a radio lecture is nothing!"

Suddenly, abruptly, a thousand questions poured in on him. Jubilantly he answered what he could, told what he thought—and then brought order. "The battle's still on, men—we've still got to find out how to use this, now we've got it. I have an idea—that there's a lot more. I know what I'll get this time. Now help me remake this apparatus so we don't broadcast the thing."

At once, ten times the former pace, work was done. On the radio, news was sent out that Kendall was on the right track after all. In two hours the apparatus had been vastly altered, it was in the final stage, and an entirely different sort of field set up. Again they watched as Buck applied the power.

The atostor hummed—but no strange tricks of matter happened this time. The more concentrated, altered field was, as Buck was to find out later, "Uncertainty of the Second Degree." It was molecular uncertainty. In a field a foot and a half in diameter, Buck saw the thing created—and suddenly a brilliant green-blue flame shot up, and a great dark cloud of terrible, red-brown deadly vapor. Then an instant later, Kendall had opened the relay. Gasping, the men ran from the laboratory, shutting the deadly fumes in. "N2O4" gasped Morton, the chemist, as they reached safety. "It's exothermic—but it formed there!"

In that instant, Kendall grasped the meaning the choking fumes carried. "Molecular uncertainty!" he decided. "We're going back—we're getting there—"

He altered the apparatus again, added another atostor in series, reduced the size of his sphere of forces—of strange chaos of uncertainty. Within—little was certain. Without—the laws of nature applied as ever.

Again the apparatus was started, cautiously this time. Only a strange jumbled ionization appeared this time, then a slow, rising blue flame began to creep up, and burn hot and blue. Buck looked at it for a moment, then his face grew tense and thoughtful. "Devin—give me a half-dollar." Blankly, Devin reached in his pocket, and handed over the metal disc. Cautiously Buck Kendall tossed it toward the sphere of force. Instantly there was a flash of flame, soundless and soft-colored. Then the silver disc was outlined in light, and swiftly, inevitably crumbling into dust so fine only a blue haze appeared. In less than two seconds, the metal was gone. Only the dense blue fog remained. Then this began to go, and the leaping blue flame grew taller, and stronger.

"We're on the track—I'm going to stop here, and calculate. Bring the data—"

Kendall shut off the machine, and went to the calculation room. Swiftly he selected already prepared graphs, graphs of the math he had worked on. Devin came soon, and others. They assembled the data and with tables and arithmetical machines turned it into graphs.

Then all these graphs were fed into the machine. There were curves, and sine-curves, abrupt breaking lines—but the answer that came when all were compounded was a perfect diagram of a flight of four steps, descending in unequal treads to zero.

Kendall looked at it for long minutes. "That," he said at length, "is what I expected. There are four degrees of uncertainty, we generated 'Uncertainty of the First Degree,' 'Mass Uncertainty,' when we started. That, as here shown, takes little energy concentration. Then we increased the energy concentration and got 'Uncertainty of the Second Degree,' 'Molecular Uncertainty.' Then I added more power, and reduced the field, and got 'Uncertainty of the Third Degree'—'Atomic Uncertainty.' There is 'Uncertainty of the Fourth Degree.' It is barely attainable with our atostors. It is—utter uncertainty.

"In the First Degree, the laws of mass action fail, the great broad-reaching laws. In the Second Degree, the laws of the molecules, a finer organization, break down, and anything can happen in chemistry. In the Third Degree, the laws of atomic physics break down slowly. The atom is tough. It is very compact, and we just barely attained the concentration needed with that apparatus. But—in the Third Degree, when the Atomic Laws break down into utter uncertainty, the atoms break, and only hydrogen can exist. That was the blue flame.

"But the Fourth Degree—there is no law whatsoever, nothing in all the Universe can exist. It means—the utter destruction and release of the energy of matter!" Kendall paused for a moment. "We have won, with this. We need only make up this apparatus—and maybe make it into a weapon. You know, in the Fourth Degree, nothing in all the Universe could resist, deflect, or control it, if launched freely, and self-maintaining. I think that might be done. You see, no law affects it, for it breaks down the law. Magnetism cannot attract or repel it because magnetic fields cannot exist; there is no law of magnetic force, where this field is.

"And you know, Devin, how I have analyzed and duplicated their magnetic ball-fields. This should be capable of formation into a ball-field.

"We need only make it up now. We will install it in the 'S Doradus' and the 'Cepheid' as a weapon. We need only install it as an energy source here. Let us start."

Chapter XII

Buck Kendall with a slow smile, looked out of the port in the thick metal wall. The magnetic shield of the Lunar Fort was washed constantly with the fires of exploding magnetic bombs. The smile spread broader. "My friends," he said softly, "you can pull from now till doomsday as far as I'm concerned, and you won't even disturb us now." He looked back over his shoulder into the power room. A hunched bulk, beautifully designed and carefully finished, the apparatus that created 'Uncertainty of the Fourth Degree' was destroying matter, and creating by its destruction terrific electric fields. These fields were feeding the magnetic shield now. Under the present drain, the machine was not noticeably working. In fact, Kendall was a bit annoyed. He had tested out the energy generating properties of this machine, trying to find a limit. He had found there was no limit. The great copper conductors, charged with the same atostor force that was used in the mercury fuel, were perfect conductors, they had not heated. But the eleven thousand tons of discharged mercury metal had been completely charged in just a bit better than eleven minutes. The pumps wouldn't force it through the charging apparatus any faster than that.

Two weeks more had passed, while the "S Doradus" and the "Cepheid" were fitted out with the new apparatus Buck had designed. They were almost ready to start now.

McLaurin came down the corridor, and stopped near Kendall. He too smiled at the Miran's attempts. "They've got a long way to go, Buck."

"They're going a long way. Clear back home—and we'll be right along. I don't think they can outdistance us."

"I still don't see why you couldn't use one of those Uncertainty conditions—the First Degree perhaps, and annihilate our inertia."

"You can't control Uncertainty. By its essential character it's beyond control."

"What's that Fourth Degree machine of yours—the material energy—if it isn't controlled and utilized Uncertainty?"

"It's utter and utterly uncontrolled Uncertainty. The matter within that field breaks down to absolutely nothing. Within, no law whatsoever applies, but fortunately, outside the old laws of physics apply—and we can gather and use the energy which is released outside, though nothing can be done inside. Why, think, man, if I could control that Uncertainty, I could do anything at all, absolutely anything. It would be a world as unreasonable as a bad dream. Think how unreasonable those manifestations we first got were!"

"But can't you get any control at all?"

"Very little. Anyway, if I could get inertialess conditions at will, I'd be afraid of them. They'd make chemical reactions impossible in all probability—and life is chemical. Two atoms must come into more or less violent contact before a union takes place, and cannot if they have neither momentum nor inertia.

"Anyway—why worry. I can't do it, because I can't control this thing. And we have the extra-space drive."

"How does that darned thing work? Can't you drop the math and tell me about it?"

Kendall smiled. "Not too readily. Remember first, as to the driving system, that it works on the fabric of space. Space is, in the physical sense, a fabric woven of the threads of lines of force from every body in the universe, made up of fields and forces. It is elastic, and can transmit strains. But anything that can transmit strains, can be strained against. With the tremendous field intensities available by the material engines, I can get such fields as will 'dig their toes' into space and push.

"That's the drive itself. It is accelerationless, because it enfolds us, and acts equally on every atom of us. By maintaining in addition a slight artificial gravity—thanks also to the intensity of those material engine fields—we can be comfortable, while we accelerate at tremendous rates.

"That is, I think, at least allied to the Stranger's system. For the high-speed drive, I do in fact use the Uncertainty. I can control it in a certain sense by determining its powers, and the limits of uncertainty, whether First, Second, Third or Fourth Degree. It advances in jumps—but on a finer plotting of the curve, you can see that each jump represents a vast series of smaller jumps. That is, there is Class A, B, C, D, and so forth Uncertainty of the First Degree. Now Class A First Degree Uncertainty involves only the deepest, broadest principles. Only they break down. One of these is the law of the speed of light.

"I'm sure that isn't the system the Strangers use, but I'm also sure there's no limit to the speed we can get."

"Doesn't that wreck your drive system?"

"No, because gravity and the fields I use in driving are First Degree Uncertainties of the higher classes.

"But at any rate, it will work. And—I suspect you came to say you were ready to go."

"I did." McLaurin nodded.

"Still stick to your original plan?"

McLaurin nodded. "I think it's best. You follow those fellows back to their system in the 'S Doradus' and I'll stay here in the 'Cepheid' to protect the system. They may need some time to get out of the place here. And remember, we ought to be as decent as they were. They didn't bother the transports leaving Jupiter when they came in, only attacked the warships. We're bound to do the same, but we'll have to keep a watch on them, nonetheless. So you go on ahead."

They started down the corridor, and came presently to the huge locks where the "S Doradus" and the "Cepheid" were berthed. The super-ships lay cold and gray now, men swarming in and out with last-minute supplies. Air, water, spare parts, bedding and personal equipment. Douglass, Cole, and most of the laboratory staff would go with Kendall when he followed the Strangers home. Devin and a few of the most advanced physicists would stay with McLaurin in case of need.

An hour later the "S Doradus" rose gently, soundlessly from her berth, and floated out of the open lock-door. The "Cepheid" followed her in five seconds. Still under the great screen of the fort, the lashing, coruscating colors of the magnetic bombs and the magnetic screen flashed and was iridescent. The "S Doradus" poked her great nose gently through the screen, and an instant later her titanically powerful, material-engine effortlessly discharged a great magnetic bomb, sent with the combined power of five atomic-powered interstellar ships. The two ships separated now, the "Cepheid" under McLaurin flashing ahead with sudden, terrific acceleration toward Mars, whispering through space at a speed that made it undetectable, faster than light. The "S Doradus" journeyed out leisurely toward the fleet of forty-seven Miran ships.

Gresth Gkae saw the "S Doradus" and as he watched the steady progress, felt sudden fear at his heart. The ship seemed so certain—

At a distance of thirty thousand miles, Kendall stopped. Magnetic bombs were washing his screen continuously now, seeking to exhaust the ship as all the great ships beyond poured their energy against it. A slow smile spread over Kendall's mouth as he heard the gentle hum of the barely working material-engine. Carefully he aligned the nose UV beam of the "S Doradus" on the nearest of the Miran ships. Then he depressed a switch.

There was no ion-release before the force-mirror now. Just a jet of gas whirling into a half-inch field of "Uncertainty of the Fourth Degree." The matter vanished instantly in released energy so stupendous that the greatest previous UV beams had been harmless things by comparison. Material energy maintained the mirror forces. Material energy gave the power that was released. And only material energy could have stood up before it. Thirty thousand miles away, a Miran ship flamed instantaneously into inconceivable incandescence, vanishing almost in blue-violet light of terrific intensity. The ship reeled away, a half-molten wreck.

The beam spotted two more ships before it winked out. Then Kendall began sending bombs. He moved up to within 2000 miles that his aim might be accurate. They were bombs of "Uncertainty of the Third Degree," the Uncertainty of atomic law in bomb form. One hit the nose of the nearest ship, and a sphere five feet in diameter glowed mistily blue for a moment. Then very easily, the matter that formed the wall of the cruiser began to run and change, and presently there was only a hole, and an expanding cloud of gas. Three more flowed toward it—and the hole enlarged, and another hole appeared in a bulkhead behind.

Kendall made a change. For the first time there came the staccato bark of the material engine under strain, as it fashioned the terrific fields of "Uncertainty of the Ultimate Degree." Abruptly they leapt out, invisible till they entered a magnetic screen, then run over with opalescent light as the energy of the field was sucked into them and released.

It struck the nose of a ship—a field no larger than an apple—

A titanic gout of energy burst out that was soundless in space. The ship suddenly opened back, opened like the peel of a banana, till a little nub remained at the further end, and the metal flaps dropped back across and behind it dejectedly. A second ship was struck, and it was struck on one side, so that it was shattered like a spent firecracker.

Then the Miran fleet vanished in speed.

Kendall followed them. "I think," he said with a grin, "they tried to use their radio beam, but it spread too much to do anything at that distance. And they used their rotating magnetic field, which we couldn't feel. And their crumbler ray too, of course. I wonder—are they headed only for Jupiter? No—no, they've passed it!"

Faster than light, faster than energy could follow through space, or Uncertainty Bombs pursue, the Mirans were fleeing for home. They knew now that only in speed lay safety. Already they knew that a similar ship had appeared off Jupiter, and, after wiping out the Phobos and Mars stations with one bomb each, had cleared the Jovian Satellites with equal terrible efficiency.

In one of the fleeing ships was a broken, tired old man, and his staff. Gresth Gkae looked back at the blank, distorted space behind them, at the swiftly dwindling sun, and spoke. "I was at fault, my friends. Jarth has spoken. They are the stronger and the wiser race. Farth Skalt has shown you—they use space fields of intensity 100. That means the energy of the ultimate destruction. Jarth used us as his instrument of testing, only to drive and stimulate that race. I do not—nay. There is no doubt now, for look."

Plainly visible, rapidly overtaking them, the "S Doradus" appeared sharp, and luminous on the jet of distorted space.

"We cannot escape, my friends. Shall we return to Sthor or remain in space, lost?"

"Let us deflect our course—at least he may not know our destination." The interstellar ship turned very slightly in her course. Plainly they saw the "S Doradus" flash on, in a straight line, headed for distant, red-glowing Mira. Gresth Gkae watched, and shrugged. Silently he put the ship back on its course, at its utmost speed. Parallel with them, near to them, the "S Doradus" flashed on. Day after day, the two hurled through space faster than light. Gradually Mira brightened, and at last became a disc.

Gresth Gkae slowed his ships, and Kendall, watching, slowed to match his speed. Five billion miles from Sthor, they had reached normal space speeds. Viciously the Miran fleet attacked the lone ship from Earth. Their rays, their bombs, their every weapon was flaming. Great interstellar ships flashed suddenly into speeds greater than that of light, seeking to ram and destroy the smaller ship. The "S Doradus" flashed into equal or greater speed, and eluded them.

Kendall had determined now, which was the leader's ship.

Gresth Gkae watched dully as his ships attempted to destroy the single, small ship. He sighed in resignation, and turned to walk back to the chapel aboard the ship. One last prayer to Jarth—

Gresth Gkae stopped abruptly. The great ship was lurching strangely. Men shouted sudden, frightened cries. The clanking and thud of relays sounded, the shrill of alarms. Then the alarms stopped, and suddenly the whole great ship vibrated to an infinitely deep voice speaking in perfect Sthorian. The voice remarked solemnly, in great, vibrant tones, that they would certainly receive news presently from the Expeditions. It went on for some seconds to discuss the conditions as reported in the new system. Then it stopped abruptly. An electric motor just above Gresth Gkae's head suddenly hummed into action without reason or power connection. Almost simultaneously he heard the shouts of startled men as the great lock doors began to open into space of their own accord, bulkhead doors slipped shut as the roar of escaping air echoed in the ship.

Then it was all over. Gresth Gkae ran to the control room. The Mirans there looked up at him with drawn faces.

"The instruments—Gresth Gkae—the instruments. The instruments read impossible things, the motors worked without reason, the fields fluctuated—the atomic engines stopped and the magnetic shield broke down and gripped part of the ship instead!" reported the bewildered pilot.

"I do not know—some strange weapon of—" began the old scientist. Something luminous and huge twisted suddenly through space toward them, a bomb of "Uncertainty of the First Degree." It wrapped the ship silently—and again strange things happened. Abruptly the ship started whirling violently, yet without centrifugal force. The heavens wheeled crazily, and turned about three axes simultaneously. There was no gyroscopic effect to hold them!

Gradually the thing died out. Then a great field seemed to catch the ship, and hurl it away from its companions. Abruptly the pilot applied all his power to pull free. In vain.

Gresth Gkae shook his head slowly, and raised the pilot's hands from the board. "Let them do as they will. I think they mean us no real harm, Thart Kralt. They can, we know, destroy us in an instant. Perhaps he wants us to go somewhere with him"—Gresth Gkae smiled sadly—"and anyway, we can do nothing."

For nearly a billion miles the great ship was hurled through space at tremendous normal-space velocity. Then abruptly it was halted, without a sign of strain or hurt. The great twenty-foot UV beam on the nose of the "S Doradus" broke into glowing gentle red light. It flashed twice. There was a pause. Then it flashed four times. A long wait. Then three times, a pause and nine times. A wait. Four times, a pause, sixteen times. Then it stopped.

A slow smile of ineffable joy spread over Gresth Gkae's face. "Jarth Be Praised. He can destroy, but does not wish to. Ah, Thart Kralt, turn your spotlight toward him, and flash it twenty-five times, for he is trying to start communications with us. Jarth is wise beyond all understanding. They were the weaker race, and they are the stronger. But also they are the better, for they could destroy, and they do not, but seek only to communicate."

Epilogue

The interstellar liner "Mirasol" settled gently to Sthor, having circled wide of Asthor, and from her hold a cargo of the heavy Jovian elements was discharged, while a mixed stream of Solarians and Mirans came from her passenger quarters.

A delegation of Mirans met the new Ambassador from Sol, Commander McLaurin, and conducted him joyfully to the Central Government Group. Beside the great buildings, a battered, scarred interstellar ship lay, her rear section a mass of great patches, rudely applied, and rudely made, mere cast metal plates.

Gresth Gkae welcomed Commander McLaurin to the Government Hall. "Your arrival today, Commander McLaurin, was most fortunate," he said in the interstellar language that had been developed, "for but yesterday Gresth Talak, my brother, arrived in his ship. Before we made that fortunate-unfortunate expedition against your system, we waited for him, and he did not come, so we knew his ship had, like others, been lost.

"He arrived only yesterday, some seventy hours ago, and explained how it had come about. He too found a solar system. But he was less fortunate than I, and while exploring this uninhabited system, far out still from the central sun, where there should have been no masses of matter, one of those rare things, a giant stony meteor that even a magnetic shield will not stop careened into the rear of his ship. Damaged badly, barely able to move, they settled to a planet. The atmosphere was breathable, the temperature mild. But while they could navigate planetary distances, they could not return, so for nearly four and a half of your years they remained there, working, working to repair their ship.

"They have done it at last. And they have returned. And best of all, after a four-year stay there, they know all they need know about that system of eleven planets. It is compact as yours, with an ultra-light sun such as yours, and four of the planets are habitable. Together we can colonize that system! It is a system of stable heat and stable light. And it is small, yet large enough. And with the devices such as your new energy has permitted, we need never fear the stony meteors again." Gresth Gkae smiled happily. "Still better—it is inhabited only by the lowest forms of life. It is too costly to both races when Jarth sees fit to stimulate them by throwing one against the other, despite the good things that may come later."

www.ingramcontent.com/pod-product-compliance
Lightning Source LLC
Chambersburg PA
CBHW031855170626
46807CB00004B/1740